STARFIGHTER COMMAND

STARFIGHTER TRAINING ACADEMY - BOOK 2

GRACE GOODWIN

GET A FREE BOOK!

JOIN MY MAILING LIST TO BE THE FIRST TO KNOW OF NEW RELEASES, FREE BOOKS, SPECIAL PRICES AND OTHER AUTHOR GIVEAWAYS.

http://freescifiromance.com

PROLOGUE

ieutenant Kassius Remeas, Planet Velerion, Eos Ground Station, Private Quarters

MY FINGERS SLID over the keypad with expert precision. Yeah, I knew they could throw me in the brig for this. My commanding officer, Captain Sponder, underestimated me, which was fine. I didn't give a shit. If he wasn't going to add me to the Starfighter Training Academy as a potential recruit, if he thought he was going to deny me the chance to become a pair-bonded Starfighter, he was wrong. I didn't *need* him to approve me. If he was going to be an asshole, then I was going to hack into the system and do it myself.

The Starfighter swirl popped up on the holographic monitor in front of me with a list of newly added candidates qualified for training. There were hundreds—people from Velerion, the Arturri moon base, every battleship and hex port.

Everyone but me.

Captain Sponder hated me with a passion I completely understood. But if I had to do everything over again so that he wasn't my nemesis, I would change nothing.

I focused on the display and analyzed the code my cipher implants allowed me to see. Connecting directly with the computer systems was a rare skill, one the Starfighter Mission Command Specialists, or MCS, coveted in their recruits.

As long as a certain captain didn't hate them, this skill would guarantee anyone a chance to enter Starfighter training. Which was great... for everyone else.

I entered yet another password, hoping to crack the final layer of security on the program. The complex system interacted directly with the alien races the rulers of Velerion were counting on to save us. Aliens training to be Starfighters on other worlds.

An orange string of code flashed across my vision before turning red and hovering there.

ACCESS: DENIED

"Asshole," I breathed but wasn't deterred. I'd been at it for two hours, trying to hack into the new training program's back-end system. I'd get there. I was deep in the code. I just needed to crack one final level of security.

There would be no stopping me. I had motivation and defiance driving me. Shuttling Starfighters from mission to mission was a solid job. Worthy. I did it with pride and skill. But it wasn't front-of-the-lines. It was support and damned important to ending the Dark Fleet once and for all, but I was underutilized. Captain Sponder knew it but wanted to see me suffer. Perhaps I deserved his wrath for all the shit I'd pulled. No doubt I was cocky. No doubt I didn't show the proper amount of respect for a superior officer.

I'd done enough to earn Sponder's raw hatred, and I'd ignored the consequences until he'd rejected me and kept me from the one thing I wanted: to be an MCS. He was holding not only me, but potentially other Starfighters back, and that didn't sit well. I could have already been paired with a graduate of the new program and be out there kicking Dark Fleet ass.

I had no idea *who* my potential match would be. Fuck, I wasn't past the last firewall. I slowed my fingers, stared at the data before me, and considered why I'd been denied access so far. The new password system had been added to keep Velerions like me out, but specifically to ensure the Dark Fleet didn't hack in, which meant there was a double parse code.

My quarters were typical for a low-ranking officer on the ground station. I was a pilot in the shuttle fleet, had been for several years thanks to Captain Sponder and the rod he had shoved so far up his ass I didn't know how he could sit in a chair. After a long day of shuttling crews and supplies between the surface of Velerion and the *Battleship Resolution*, returning to find yet another denial of promotion into the Starfighter Training Program—signed by Sponder, of course—had filled me with ice-cold determination. He'd denied me what I wanted for too long. I'd played by the rules—okay, maybe not all of them. But I'd done everything I was supposed to do, never putting what I wanted above the lives of the fighters I shuttled. Now I was tired of waiting.

Everyone but critical personnel was asleep. Just like I was supposed to be. After pulling a ten-hour flight shift, I was required to rest. It was the rule. I would, but it wasn't going to come until—

ACCESS: USER UNIDENTIFIED

I GROANED but pushed on because I was getting somewhere. I could feel it. My fingers flew again. "I'm going to get in and get matched to my pair bond. Nothing—not even a stupid triplex-split pass code—is going to stop me," I said to myself.

I held my finger over the last key as I stared at the holographic data, the line of numbers and letters. This was it. The hair on the back of my neck stood up. My fingers itched. I had it. I knew it.

I pushed the button.

ACCESS: GRANTED
    WELCOME CAPTAIN SPONDER

. . .

I ALMOST CACKLED. Not only was I going to enter my data into the training system, but I was going to make it look like Sponder himself had done it.

I spoke my command. "Enter new candidate."

I waited less than a second.

WELCOME TO THE STARFIGHTER TRAINING ACADEMY PORTAL. ENTER CANDIDATE DATA.

"YES!" I shouted, the one word bouncing off my quarter's thick walls. The holographic screen filled with instructions about what I needed to do next. I pulled in my service record.

"Lieutenant Kassius Remeas, shuttle pilot." I found my data file and confirmed its accuracy before submitting the file. I would need to complete my bio and survey, but first I had to stand and allow my body to be scanned to create my avatar. Cool. Next, the training computer would use my voice and my image to interact with my potential partner. She would see a real version of me, just as I would see a real version of her.

I stood, listened to the voice tell me what to do as every inch of me was visually imported into the training program. I would hope for a match, then train beside her. She would be a fierce, beautiful female. One who was my equal, my other half. She'd have to be skilled to train as an MCS. We would endure the simulations and welcome victory together.

When the scan was done, I dropped into my seat and got to work, eagerly giving answers to the program's questions. The avatar looked exactly like me, except it had converted my standard shuttle pilot uniform into the dark black of a Starfighter's, complete with the metallic swirl worn only by the elite.

"Damn, that looks good on you, soldier." I chuckled, answering the survey and personality questions. I didn't hold back the truth about myself. Arrogant. Aggressive. Defiant. Disobedient. I was who I was. I *would* be a Starfighter MCS.

And Captain Sponder could go fuck himself.

One Year Later...Mia Becker,
Berlin, Germany, 2:24 AM

I WAS ten minutes into the game. I was wired in, and my fingers flew over the controls. On-screen, Kassius, the Velerion hunk I'd created to be my training partner, sat in the pilot's seat looking handsome and stoic and almost real. Handsome wasn't the right word. *Hot* was better. When my friend and fellow player, Jamie, had said she had a crush on her imaginary sidekick, I hadn't laughed because I had one on mine, too.

Not a thirteen-year-old-girl boy-band kind of love, but an all-out, I-wanted-him-naked-in-my-bed

kind of craving. My vibrator got a workout as I
thought of Kass. Nightly and often twice on nights I
played the game and spent hours listening to his
voice. I knew it made me slightly crazy and a sign I
needed to date more, but no men I met matched
Kass's... everything.

The game, *Starfighter Training Academy*, was cool
and challenging, but it wasn't all that fun anymore.
Not since Jamie had won the game and went radio
silent two weeks ago. She'd literally disappeared
after celebrating her win. Jamie, Lily, and I had all
watched the cut scene finale as General Aryk
congratulated her on becoming an Elite Starfighter.
Watched when she'd accepted the pair bond to her
game-made hottie, Alexius. Sat stunned as her
screen had gone black. After that... nothing. No
Jamie when I'd tried to connect to play again. Lily
hadn't had any better luck. Our friend had just
poofed into thin air. Vanished.

Gone.

With my job in the intelligence community and
my hacking skills, I couldn't let it go. I'd accessed
places a normal person wouldn't dream of looking.
She might live on the other side of the Atlantic, but
everything in the world was online. In police files.
Tax paperwork. Employment records.

I'd even hacked Jamie's employer's database—which had been ridiculously easy—and discovered that she'd been terminated for not showing up for work. That had been over a week ago.

Searching for family had come next. It was possible she was visiting her *oma.* But no. No grandmother. No father or siblings. Only a mother who was in a prison-run rehab program. Their log showed that Jamie had not called or visited once.

"You have no idea where she is?" Lily asked through my headset as I watched her pound the side of a Dark Fleet stronghold into rubble with her giant mechanical fists. As usual we were playing together, and her destructive tendencies appeared to be opposite what I imagined when compared to her soft British accent. She was a librarian in real life but made me think of a prima ballerina swinging a sledgehammer when she played the game. Lily tore through Dark Fleet scum like a tank playing in the Starfighter Titan division.

"None," I replied. "I tracked her phone number and called. No answer. It's like she vanished off the face of the Earth." I spoke clearly into my headset as I looked to the pilot's seat on the stealth ship Kass and I were flying for this mission in the game, which I hadn't been able to beat.

Yet. But Kass—yup, I'd given him a nickname—and I got closer to winning every time. As an MCS pair, he flew the *Phantom*, which was what I had named our ship. Generally, he piloted and I sat buckled into the computer that covered the copilot's area as well as the entire rear of the cockpit, using my computer skills to hack into the Dark Fleet's systems from the complex quantum processors as he moved in so close we could have reached out and touched the enemy with our bare hands.

As I played, I spoke to Kass as if he were real, and he gave formulated responses. I even chatted when he never said anything back, as if we were truly side by side fighting the Dark Fleet. Anyone would call me crazy, but I was half in love with him.

An avatar in a video game.

An alien, no less, who was just pixels on my screen.

Sometimes he seemed more real to me than the people I worked with. Then again, my colleagues were serious and dangerous, and we all lived with a lot of secrets. They were good people, loyal. Dedicated. Lonely. People like me.

I never once fantasized about my coworkers. Never dreamed of being pushed up against the wall. Never imagined dropping to my knees and making any one of them lose their mind as my hair was tugged.

"She hasn't used her credit cards?" Lily asked, breaking me from my dirty thoughts. About an alien in a video game. Maybe Jamie was in an insane asylum and I would be joining her next.

"How would I know that?"

"Don't bother lying. I know what you do." Lily's chuckle followed as her Titan mechanical warrior—something like a *Mech Warrior* or a *Transformer* straight out of an action movie—jumped on top of a low-flying enemy shuttle and ripped off the communication panel with its powerful hands. "This the one you want?"

My eyes widened as she'd done that so easily. We'd all improved as we'd played together. Jamie had won the game first because she'd been a badass as a starfighter pilot. "Easy, Lily. There are bombs on that shuttle. They could blow."

This bomb-run mission was a new addition to the game with enemy weapons that could easily take us both out. Then it would be game over.

Our mission task—mine and Kass's—was to hover over the shuttle and remain hidden from the Dark Fleet ships' sensors, take control of that shuttle through hacking, then redirect it at the Dark Fleet's

armada and blow them all to bits, using their own
weapons against them.

"Not going to happen." Lily's Titan jumped off
the shuttle as Kass flew us in close.

"Thanks, Lily."

"Go get 'em!"

I grinned as I hacked into the shuttle's navigation
system and remotely steered it away from the planet's surface.

"You're fifteen seconds ahead of where we were
last time." Lily's voice was husky with excitement.
"You're going to bloody do it this time, Mia. You're
really going to do it!"

My gaze dropped to the timer in the lower right
corner of the screen. Fuck, yes!

My nerves were finally coming to life. I'd never
made it this far before. I held my breath. This could
be it. Final victory. Or we'd be blown up, our game
lives gone, and we'd have to start the mission over.
Again.

I might actually beat the game this time. Not Lily.
She didn't have enough experience points. She
needed to level up and tackle her final mission.

"If I do this, Lily, you're the only one of us left."

"I'm right behind you in points. It's not the same
without Jamie. And it won't be without you."

That was assuming my screen went black like Jamie's had and Lily would have to play without the two of us. She'd just have to use game-generated playing partners until she finished her final mission.

"I gave you my phone number so you have it and you can call me. I'll find Jamie."

"How are you going to do that?"

"I've got a few favors I can call in."

"In the United States?"

A reasonable question since I lived and worked in Germany.

"Yes. Among other places."

"You're scary sometimes. You know that?"

Coming from Lily, I wasn't sure whether to take that as an insult or a compliment. She was a one-woman wrecking ball in the game. And her on-screen partner, Darius, was even crazier.

"Yes. I do know that."

Nothing stopped me when I had a goal, and right now I wanted to win. However, winning this game had a downside. I didn't want to say goodbye to Kass. He was tall, dark, and handsome, of course. But he was also insanely brave, funny, and a real pain in the ass. He made me laugh and scared the hell out of me at the same time. He was arrogant and unpredictable. He was sex and danger and protection all rolled into one.

He wasn't real. I knew it, but *scheisse,* he was the one for me. I *wanted* him more than I'd ever wanted any flesh-and-blood human male. Pathetic but true. Jamie and Lily understood. In fact, Lily had once discussed purposely losing the game so we wouldn't have to give up our make-believe alien men.

I watched on-screen as Kass timed our cloaked ship's movement perfectly and dived directly beneath the wing of a Dark Fleet shuttle, their smallest, most heavily armored transport. The cloaking technology worked, and they never noticed us.

"Nice flying," I said to Kass but also pushed the button on my on-screen phrases I'd programmed in to tell him.

His deep, sexy voice rumbled through my headset in reply to the chat post. "Anything for you, love." He had about a hundred different phrases, and every single one of them made me shiver.

His accent was thick but unrecognizable, like they'd taken ancient Greek, ancient Turkish, and a little French and put them in a blender. I loved the sound of his voice.

I homed in on my screen again. The Dark Fleet

shuttle I had taken control of flew through space with erratic and unpredictable movements. Lily had made sure its communications were out so they couldn't warn their armada that I was about to steer it into the landing bay of their queen's massive warship and blow them all to hell.

"Be careful, Mia. We're close." Kass's soft warning pulled me into the game.

"There are so many of them." I'd never been this deep behind enemy lines on this mission before. Those fifteen seconds Lily and I had gained made all the difference. We were surrounded by what had to be at least half of Queen Raya's fleet... and her ship sitting like a giant target in the middle.

"Thirty seconds." Kass's alert was automatic, and I responded aloud, even though he was a computer-generated alien and wouldn't hear me.

"On it, gorgeous."

"Get 'em, Mia!" Lily's excited shout made me grind my teeth, but I didn't chastise her for the volume. She was very much on my side.

"Setting self-destruct timer." My fingers flew over my controls as I programmed the enemy shuttle's death throes, hoping it would explode after it flew deep inside the queen's command ship. The bombs would tear through every Dark Fleet ship in the area. At least, that was the idea.

I scanned my nav grid to ensure the Starfighter teams were all safely out of range of the blast. I knew how to fly this ship if I had to. Just as Kass knew how to hack enemy systems. But he was better at the flying, and I was a *lot* better at the hacking.

I waited, finger on the activation command for the shuttle's self-destruct sequence, when Kass flew our ship directly beneath the launch bay doors of the queen's warship. He held us there as I directed the enemy shuttle up over our heads and into the bay area.

The moment it cleared the doors, I activated the timer and autopilot. It would keep flying forward and land inside.

Kass's deep rumble made me squirm in my seat. "Excellent job, Starfighter."

Why did his praise make me smile and make my panties wet at the same time?

We flew away at maximum speed as I watched the countdown.

"Ten seconds," I said.

"Nine. Eight. Seven. Six. Yes, Mia! Three. Two," Lily said in my ear.

I held my breath as the screen flashed with the

explosion of Queen Raya's warship, her entire fleet lighting up like fiery dominoes in the darkness of space.

"Wow." I'd never seen such massive destruction in the game before.

What followed was no surprise. I'd seen it before, when Jamie won.

My avatar appeared, standing in a formal-looking room with high ceilings. Before mine and Kass's avatars stood a stern-looking general... and Kass was looking at me with an expression I'd never seen before. Was that desire?

God, these programmers were good.

Kass held the Starfighter emblem in his palm and extended the offering toward me like it was an engagement ring. He asked if I—I mean, if my character in the game—would accept him and be his pair-bonded fighting partner for life.

I didn't let him finish asking. My finger was already on the X button. I pressed it, and my screen went black. No more game. No more Kass. Or so I thought. This was exactly what had happened to Jamie when she beat the game.

It was my turn to find out what happened next.

ass, Pilot on Transport Shuttle XF41,
Airspace above Eos Station

"SHUTTLE XF41, this is Eos Station. Come in." The Velerion ground base comm officer hailed my shuttle. I'd just dropped a bonded pair of Starfighter Titans and a dozen ground troops at the outer grid for a training exercise. I was coming in for the day. Done.

"Eos, this is XF41. Go ahead."

"Lieutenant Remeas, you are to return to the *Battleship Resolution* immediately."

"I dropped off their team. Are you sure?"

"Orders are to return to the *Resolution* at once to

receive modified mission instructions." The ground tech's voice came through the cockpit loud and clear. Apparently I was not yet done with today's taxiing service.

"Copy that, Eos. Going back to the *Resolution.*" I replied, checking my display for speed and expected arrival time. "What are the mission modifications? Does someone else need transport?"

I was tired and needed to sleep before I could be assigned another mission. All I wanted was to take a shower and stroke off to my usual fantasy of Mia, my Starfighter training partner, yelling at me while we fought in the simulations together and taking her against the wall to silence that sharp tongue. If the new mission instructions delayed that, it might be an issue because my body was hard for her, even now, alone in space.

"Per protocol, you are to report immediately to *Battleship Resolution.* You have been reassigned to Starfighter MCS. Your partner has completed the training program and must be retrieved immediately from their home planet."

My breath caught in my throat. Holy shit. With the time delay between Velerion and Earth, the training simulations we participated in together were an odd mix of recorded messages and mission reviews. Mia would go through a training simulation and then I would be notified and load up the program to experience and participate in the mission simulation myself. I knew Mia now. Her reactions. The tone of her voice when she was exasperated with me. I assumed she was familiar with me as well, as many of the pre-recorded messages I created were spoken in the heat of battle. The new Starfighter training system was like an odd game of virtual tag. We both had to learn and make adjustments on our own before the training simulation would allow us to win as a team.

And now, we were finished. Training complete. Mia was a Starfighter and so was I.

"Lieutenant?" The comms officer at Eos Station sounded confused by my silence, but this was a lot to process. Mia was mine. I was a Starfighter MCS. Free from Sponder's control and free to make my own destiny at last.

"Shuttle X41, do you copy?"

"Yes. Earth. Mia's on Earth." I stared out the window at the blackness of space on my left and the looming Eos Station, a massive, sprawling ground complex on Velerion.

The comms officer chuckled at my rattled response.

"Congratulations, Starfighter. General Jennix is expecting you to report for duty."

It had to be real if Jennix was giving the order.

My heart started to pound, and I couldn't help the smile that spread across my face. The shuttle was empty. Ensuring the comms were off first, I shouted out my pleasure.

"Fuck, yes!"

She'd done it. *My* Mia. The female I'd been matched to for months. Who I longed to touch and craved like a drowning man needed air. Since I'd hacked my way into the training program, I'd kept the fact that I'd been partnered to a female MCS trainee a secret. From everyone. Friends didn't know. Fellow shuttle pilots either. No one. In fact, the only one I could speak to about the training program was Mia, who was *in* the simulation itself. And that conversation had been limited to the few prerecorded options available. There certainly wasn't one that said, *Finish the mission and I will reward you with my head between your thighs.*

I'd heard her voice. I'd spent hours and hours in the simulation fighting beside a recorded version of her. Yet I'd never seen a real image of her, only her avatar. Brown hair I ached to run my fingers through. Full lips. Dark eyes so intense and filled with secrets I longed to push her until that rigid control broke and she became fire under my touch. And she would burn. I saw the passion in her gaze, saw it in the way she battled next to me in our training ship, aptly named *Phantom*.

Since I was being sent to retrieve her from Earth, it meant she had not only finished the Starfighter Training Academy; she had accepted my prerecorded request to pair bond with me. Fight with me. Be mine. Forever.

When my match to Mia had occurred, I'd expected to be called into Captain Sponder's office so he could yell at me for insubordination. But that had never happened. No alarms had been raised when I'd been matched to Mia. No one had known, which only made my satisfaction sweeter. There were so many around the universe using the training program, I figured there was no way any officer in the Velerion fleet would have time to monitor them all, which meant I'd flown under the proverbial radar.

At least until now, when a recruit from a far-off planet actually finished and impacted the current role of someone like me. Since Mia had graduated and was now a Starfighter MCS, that meant I was one, too. It also meant I'd meet her in person. Soon get her beneath me. Tell her how much that bossy mouth made me crazy. I wouldn't have to get off to thoughts of her. I'd get *her* off.

And thank her for ensuring I now outranked Captain Sponder and his hatred.

The grin that spread across my face was unavoidable.

"Starfighter, you have not altered course to the *Battleship Resolution.*"

Starfighter. He called me *Starfighter*. Fuck yes!

"Is there a problem?" The comm officer from Eos Station must have been monitoring my position on their sensors.

"No, Eos. No problem. On my way. XF41 out," I said once I had my voice and emotions under control. No, my emotions weren't under control. I'd done it. Well, I'd hacked into the system and added myself. No, I hadn't done much except that and partner with the most amazing, smart, and talented human. She'd worked her ass off in all the simulations. *We* had. I'd been with her on mission after mission, watched as she'd failed. As she'd succeeded. Learned. Grew. Because she'd done all that, I'd been able to enhance my flying skills, tie in my own computer abilities to hers. Every simulation and training session we each completed had to relived and completed by the other.

The long distance between Earth and Velerion made the training more difficult, but somehow we had become a powerful pair. So skilled that as far as I'd heard, Mia and I were only the second pair to complete the new training program.

Word had spread fast about the newest Starfighter pilot, about how Jamie Miller, a human female, had become the first recruit from Earth. If I was getting word of Mia's success, then everyone at Eos Station would have heard. And know that she had chosen me.

Definitely.

Mia was it. The second Starfighter, but this time a Mission Control Specialist would come to Velerion instead of a pilot. *My* MCS. I would see her in person. Talk to her. Hear her laughter. Touch her. Fuck her. Now she was mine.

———

Mia, Treptowers, Federal Criminal Police Office (Bundeskriminalamt (BKA)), Berlin, Germany

. . .

I STARED at the nearest screen, one of six, and watched the data change. The chart shifted in real time, and I was able to analyze and make changes swiftly to the data I'd requested for my latest project.

They might have stuck me behind a desk—as I deserved after the clusterfuck my so-called informant had made of our last investigation—but I was determined to be useful, to prove myself. Getting over the two agent deaths my bad information had caused? That would take longer.

Maybe they were right about me. Maybe I should have chosen a profession outside of law enforcement. Like knitting. Or gardening. At least then the only deaths I would be responsible for would be plants.

And who could make a damn plant grow anyway? In fact, the stupid plant I had on my desk was dead, the brown, crispy leaves taunting me with yet another failure.

Damn it.

I picked up the small pot and dropped the whole mess into the garbage bin under my desk. Gone. Next.

The windows of my office afforded me a view of the city's charming mix of new and old buildings, but heavy rain streaked the glass and a thick fog

obscured all but the post-war offices across the
street. My mood matched the weather. The night
before, I'd finished *Starfighter Training Academy.* Lily
and I had watched as I was congratulated by the
Mission Control Commander, General Jennix. Her
avatar showed a woman with black hair streaked
with silver at the temples, focused hazel eyes and a
back so straight I wondered if she was a cyborg with
a metal spine. But the sound of her voice through
my speakers had been almost eager. I remembered
the same screen, the same words spoken when Jamie
had completed the game, although a different
general had welcomed her. Perhaps because she'd
been a pilot instead of MCS? I had no idea, but I
distinctly remembered a tall, dark, and handsome
man. General Aryk?

Jamie had accepted the game's ceremonial
bonding to Alexius of Velerion with mine and Lily's
coaxing. The first time we'd all seen the final cut
scene, the pair bonding questions had been exciting
if a bit weird. Jamie might have hesitated that day.
Not me. I'd pushed the X button before Lily even
prompted me. Maybe because I'd won after Jamie
and knew what to expect, the oddly personal nature
of the scene had seemed less daunting. Or maybe I
just wanted Kass so badly that accepting a fictional

bond with a man was the most exciting thing I'd done in months.

My gut instinct insisted that accepting this pair bond with a fictional alien, that beating the game was somehow the key to finding Jamie. I was insane, definitely, to think that, but I needed to know what had happened to her. If following in her footsteps led me to her whereabouts, I'd do it.

Because I was desperate. I'd exhausted every legitimate option I had. The data I was watching scroll by on my monitor offered me no help. I did my work, but I had also used my inside skills and connections at the Federal Criminal Police Office to search for one Jamie Miller of Baltimore, Maryland, in the United States. With zero success.

"Mia?" A colleague from the data lab knocked on the door to my office.

"Yes?"

"Sorry. The whole thing's gone. Scrubbed and overwritten."

"*Scheisse*," I muttered, swearing under my breath. The game, the data, and my game console's hard drive had been wiped clean? "Are you sure?"

He rolled his eyes at me as he placed the unassembled console on the seat of the chair in front of my desk. "I don't make mistakes, Becker."

Not like you. I don't get people killed.

I could practically hear the accusation in his tone, read behind the lines. But I didn't blame him for his rage. One of the agents who'd died had been his friend. And mine. But no one seemed to remember that.

"Sorry. Stupid question. Thank you."

He nodded and left, softly closing the door to my office behind him. Of course he was sure. He was very good at his job. I was talented with computer code and with reading people. But no one could hack into a system that had no data to break into. Not even me.

If this blackout was a game defect or a recall issue, I had heard nothing of it. I'd spent hours in gamer chats since Jamie had disappeared, searching for anyone else who had managed to beat the game, with no luck. I was cranky. The exhilaration of winning had been short-lived. Just like with Jamie, my screen had gone black after I'd accepted the role as Starfighter MCS. After I'd accepted Kass as my pair-bonded, lifetime fighting partner.

It was as if I had blown up my game with the push of a single button. There was nothing left of my score, my avatar. Or Kass.

I couldn't even start the game over.

I'd tossed and turned all night, frustrated by the fact that if the game was dead, then I wouldn't hear Kass's grumbling voice ever again. Thank goodness I'd taken photos of him on the gaming screen and saved them to my phone like a lovesick teenager. Not that I would ever admit that fact to another human being. But I'd taken some very personal time staring at that image of Kass while in my bed.

So far I'd spent the day tackling my new punishment projects—as I liked to think of them—and even more time scouring the system for clues about Jamie's disappearance. There was nothing. Now the analysts had confirmed what I already knew in my heart.

Everything was gone. Wiped. Destroyed. The *Phantom*. The missions I'd completed. And Kass, the imaginary man I'd spent the last few months obsessing over.

I was an idiot to become emotionally attached to a fictional character. But there wasn't much room for dating in my line of work, and Kass had somehow become more real to me than any man I'd ever dated. Which was no surprise if a few dinners followed by casual sex could be called dating. Eventually the men I "dated" all grew tired of my secrecy. I didn't tell them who I worked for or what I did. Most of them didn't even know my real name.

Then I'd started the game and saw Kass, and my interest in dating had stopped completely. No one held my interest but him.

"Stop moping, you big baby," I scolded myself and tried to focus on work. Two long hours remained until I could go home and laze around the apartment. I'd spend another sleepless night with no update on Jamie, no game time with Kass to soothe my nerves, and no idea what to do next.

I was the expert in getting answers. Yet I had none, which made me even more cranky.

All I knew was that I missed my friend. I missed playing the game I'd won and then broken. I missed Kass, a video game–created alien that didn't even exist.

Without doubt, I worked too much. I needed to get out more. Meet real people. Learn a new hobby. Spelunking. Pretzel making. Hell, even go on some kind of adventure vacation.

Anything as long as I didn't have to admit to anyone I was upset and frustrated because I was lusting after a computer-generated avatar and my only link to him had blown up.

My desk phone beeped. I picked up the receiver. "Yes?"

"Ms. Becker? This is the front desk. There's someone here to see you."

This building had super-tight security. From key fobs for all areas to retinal scans for access in others. But I also wasn't expecting anyone. I had no outside appointments, and my only friends were... well, one was missing and the other lived in London. I frowned.

"Did they give a name?"

"Kassius Remeas."

 *ia*

"What?"

I blinked and my heart went erratic. Was someone making fun of me? No. How could the front desk staff know I even played the game? We only offered quick hellos in the morning when I arrived. They certainly weren't aware I obsessed over my MCS partner. No one in Germany knew.

"He said his name is Kassius Remeas."

"Is this a joke?" If so, I was not amused.

"No. There is a gentleman here who asked specifically for you. He insisted you would know him."

What the hell?

"Send him to conference room three. I'll be down in a moment. Thank you."

"Of course. My pleasure."

I put the phone in the cradle and popped to my feet, my desk chair rolling backward.

Kass wasn't here. The very idea was a joke. He wasn't *real.*

As I had not discussed my gaming habits with anyone at work, someone must have set up surveillance equipment inside my apartment. "*Sohn einer Hündin!*"

I knew *Starfighter Training Academy* was a popular game all over the world, but I had no idea the game had already infiltrated Earth's culture to such a degree. Then again, I never went out these days, so I didn't know a lot about pop culture at the moment. I did know that curiosity was killing me and I could not ignore the chance to see Kass one more time—even an actor dressed up to look like him. I would enjoy looking at the man, and hunting down whoever had sent him—and put surveillance in my apartment—even more.

Someone out there knew exactly how obsessed I was. I had become heartsick and pathetic in the hours since I'd beaten the game. Pathetic. Capital *P.*

Weak. Given someone a vulnerability to use against me.

I put a call in to our security teams. "This is Becker. I need an apartment sweep as soon as possible."

"Copy that. What do you think the odds are we'll find something?"

"One hundred percent."

"Yes, ma'am. I'll have a team dispatched in ten minutes."

"Thank you. Please let me know immediately." The tech teams would search my apartment top to bottom. Whatever surveillance equipment had been installed would be gone. But that didn't help me with the current situation. Who had sent someone here using Kass's name? And what the hell did they hope to gain? This made no sense. I would be stuck sitting behind a desk for God knew how long. I'd been removed from most of my cases. What was the play? And why now?

I waited for the call. Ten minutes felt like an eternity. Twenty. Thirty.

I was about to pull my hair out when my phone rang. "Mia Becker."

"Your apartment is clean, ma'am. We're finished."

"What? You didn't find anything? Nothing?"

"No, ma'am. We can look again if you're sure. But my teams is experienced and efficient."

"No, thank you. I appreciate your work."

"Not a problem." The line went dead, and I discovered I was shaking.

If no one had bugged my apartment, then how the hell did they know about Kass? Maybe Jamie had been kidnapped and interrogated? Had they planted surveillance in Lily's apartment in London? Lily was a librarian, spent hours dusting off ancient books. And Jamie was a delivery driver, not James Bond. This made zero sense.

I wiped my hands down my black pants, my palms suddenly damp. The elevator ride to the first floor felt like an eternity as I made my way to the meeting room I'd instructed this Kassius Remeas be escorted to. My high heels clicked rhythmically against the hard floor, and I straightened my suit jacket, buttoned it as if I were putting on armor. I arrived to stare at the closed door, hands shaking.

Waited.

Before I could open the door, it flew open, smacking against the wall and bouncing back a few inches. I jumped, startled. Then I stared. And stared.

There, standing before me, was a *really* good likeness of Kass.

Someone had gone all out. This guy had the same dark hair. The same crooked smile. The same small scar under his left eye. The same dark brown eyes. The same fucking dimples that made him look like a mischief-making, super-sexy space pirate. He was dressed head to toe in black, the cut and tailoring exactly matching the in-game uniforms of a Starfighter MCS, but he had no adornments or anything else that indicated he was in the military. Any military. And fool that I was, my gaze darted to his chest to look for the Starfighter insignia. Which was there. Black on black, but the damn swirl was there. I even recognized the buckles on his boots.

What the hell? This space alien uniform was absurd. Laughable, which meant I was the brunt of the joke now for the half second that my heart leaped and my body tightened as if he was real. Two heartbeats later the stupid organ ached ten times more than it had before as the leap of joy crashed back into the pit of despair. Because this man looked exactly like Kassius Remeas, in the flesh.

So, was this man a model? Maybe the game developer had placed him in front of a green screen and based the avatar of Kassius Remeas on him.

Maybe I was hallucinating and a pimply-faced teen with a half-grown mustache and gangly legs was staring back at me. Perhaps the stress of the job had finally sent my mental health into a tailspin.

But I couldn't tear my eyes off him. Fuck that, I couldn't blink. Or breathe.

"Mia Becker." He didn't say more but inspected me with the same intense scrutiny I gave him.

I wasn't going to call him Kass. It would hurt too much. Uttering that one syllable meant that I was buying into the entire joke. And I felt that it was all on me.

Without tearing his gaze away, he pulled me into the room and shoved the door shut behind me. He even turned the lock. The sounds of the reception desk, security checkpoints, and scattered voices dropped away, leaving us very much alone. The room was sealed and searched every morning for surveillance equipment. The walls were thick, and there were no windows.

I still didn't speak, and he narrowed his eyes. Then he closed the distance between us, gently placed his hands on each side of my head, and kissed me.

Scheisse.

For a second I froze because a paid actor or

model—a complete stranger—was kissing me. With soft lips. With a need I felt seep through his fingers, his mouth. Every inch of him radiated desire. For me.

Damn, he was good. I almost believed what his lips were telling me.

I whimpered because it was one hell of a kiss. He took advantage when I opened my mouth, to plunge his tongue deep and take. To claim.

His hands angled my head as he wanted, taking us deeper into... a connection. A fusion that was more than just our lips and tongues touching.

I didn't even know we'd moved until my back pressed into the wall and his hard body leaned into me. I felt how hard he was. *Everywhere.*

I had no idea how long we kissed, but when he finally lifted his head, I realized his hand was beneath my shirt and his rough palm cupped my breast.

"Mia," he said again. This time the rasp was deeper. Darker. "I found you." He spoke in English, which confused me further but I responded in kind.

"Wow." I licked my lips, and his gaze dropped to the motion. "I don't know who you are, but you kiss really well."

The corner of his mouth tipped up. "I am

Kassius Remeas of Velerion, as you well know, Starfighter MCS Mia Becker of Earth. I am your partner and pair-bonded mate. You had better not greet all your visitors this way."

He looked down to where his thumb was moving slowly back and forth beneath my silk blouse.

I was wet. Achy. Needy for this stranger.

"Thank you for the fun because... sure, you look just like him. I'll even give you a bonus for excellent kissing, but if you would like to keep your hands, you need to take them both off me. Now."

He slowly shook his head as a grin spread across his lips. He called my bluff. I didn't want to hurt him. At least not yet.

"I'm just getting started. We've been fighting side by side for months, and I've been waiting to silence that sassy mouth all this time."

I eyed him now. Wary. He wasn't dropping his game, but I wasn't quite ready to knee him in the balls either. He looked like Kass. He sounded like Kass. He was wearing a Starfighter MCS uniform so detailed even the boots matched. But the leap my hopeful heart wanted to make was impossible.

"You don't believe me," he said, studying me closely.

"That an avatar from a game I've been playing is

actually a real person, a real alien, who's come to my office to kiss me? And that you are from another planet but you just happen to speak English?" I played *Starfighter Training Academy* in English since Jamie and Lily spoke it. German was my first language, but I was fluent in both. For an alien, he spoke English really well.

"I learned your language while playing the game. I am not well versed. And I did not come here to kiss you," he said; then his cheeks darkened. "That is a lie. I have ached to kiss you for months."

"Who sent you? How long have you been watching my apartment?"

"General Jennix approved your retrieval. I know nothing of your home. I would very much like to see it before we leave."

"Leave?"

"Yes. We must go to Velerion. They need you, Mia. As I do."

Oh hell. He was good. His gaze locked on to mine with utmost sincerity. His face held not one hint of a smile, nor of confusion. He seemed perfectly functional and coherent. Which meant either he believed what he was saying, or he was the best liar I'd ever spoken to. Ever.

"This is crazy. What are you talking about? Who are you, really? How did you find out where I work?"

"I am your Kassius. We are a pair bond. I've come here to take you to the *Battleship Resolution*. General Jennix is awaiting our arrival. She is very excited to welcome a Starfighter MCS pair to her command." His gaze raked over my face, and he seemed content to cup my breast. He growled. "First, though, I need to fuck you to take the edge off the need I know we've both had all this time."

My naughty side loved his dirty talk. So did the rest of me. The feminist within insisted I should slap him, because a stranger coming in and saying he was going to fuck me deserved a solid slap. Or knee to the 'nads.

But I felt safe with this guy. Aroused. "This is insane," I whispered.

"It is not. You call the *Starfighter Training Academy* a game, which is clearly a problem for the Velerion design team to rectify. In truth, the system is a complex and difficult training program, and you completed it. *We* completed it. Together."

I shook my head, hoping to clear some of the fog his kiss had created. "No. Who sent you? What do you want?"

"You, *my Mia*."

How had he known that endearment? Even if someone had planted cameras and mics in my apartment, they would not have known Kass called me that. No one knew. His voice, his verbal responses were only ever heard through my headset. I didn't use the captioning feature. Words floating across the screen distracted me. His name had flashed on the screen for a camera to see. So had the Starfighter uniforms—every detail of him was perfect. But no one knew Kass called me that, no one but the imaginary computer avatar on my now-defunct gaming system. This couldn't be real. Could it? "What did you just call me?"

"My Mia. I have called you this many times, love." He grinned and kissed my forehead. "Especially during that mission to Xenon where you single-handedly crushed an entire squadron of Dark Fleet drones."

Holy shit. That mission had been months ago, back in the early days. That was the first mission where he'd used the endearment. I remembered well because everything female in me had practically melted the first time I'd heard that sexy growl say my name like that. My Mia. So hot. So sexy. So him.

"Kass?"

"You accepted your role as a Starfighter MCS. You accepted our pair bond. As I have. The bond has been recorded in the Hall of Records on Velerion. You are mine and I am yours. I have been waiting for you."

I have been waiting for you. God, a sexy warrior telling a woman that, one whose hand was still on her breast. It was a panty-melting sentence that I actually believed because I'd been waiting for him, too.

I had.

I was sappy. A dreamer. Crazy.

Whatever.

His. Hand. Was. On. My. Breast.

I rolled my hips into his, feeling every inch of his hard length.

He groaned. "I need you."

"I'm crazy for saying this, but I think I have an idea of how much."

His mouth tipped up at the corner, and his eyes darkened, turned molten.

I believed him. My instincts and logic were both in agreement. Far-fetched? Maybe. But I lived my life by the theory of Ockham's razor: *the simplest explanation was usually the right one.* No one on Earth had any reason to go to all this trouble to pull a joke on me. No one. Regarding aliens, I'd had my suspicions for years. Assuming they *did* exist, then there were his clothes. His face. His voice. His name. And the clincher, Jamie's disappearance...

"Jamie Miller. She won the game. Did Alex come for her, too? Is that why she disappeared?" It was so obvious now. A lost puzzle piece that had been found. It made complete sense. If Kass was here for me, then Alex, the avatar Jamie had chosen to be her fighting partner in her game, must have come for her. I had to know.

He nodded once. "Starfighter Pilot Jamie Miller is famous among the Velerions. She was the first Starfighter from Earth and has already saved many lives and faced down Queen Raya. Her pair bond, Alexius, retrieved her as I have now come for you. Starfighters Jamie and Alexius serve under General Aryk on Moon Base Arturri."

I relaxed against the wall. I'd looked everywhere... on Earth. I wasn't losing my touch at hacking and tracking. The best intelligence gathering systems in Europe had not failed. I had been looking in the wrong place. On the wrong *planet*.

"I... we, you and I, worked with her on her final training mission. I saw her accept her role with General Aryk and the pair bond with Alexius. You are telling me he came to Earth to retrieve her? And take her to outer space? To Velerion? Velerion is real?"

"Yes. Exactly. Now you understand." He lowered his head and placed a line of soft kisses along my jaw. If I hadn't been leaning against the wall, I would have fallen over. Body melting on the outside, mind reeling on the inside.

Holy shit. It was real. "Jamie is in space? On Velerion?" One more time. I had to hear it one. More. Time.

"On Arturri, the moon base where Starfighter pilots are stationed. She has adapted well, by all reports."

"You haven't seen her?"

Kass shook his head, taking the opportunity to move his lips to the opposite side of my jaw. "Only on official reports. After her escape from Queen Raya's warship, General Aryk sent excerpts of their debrief to all pilots so we would know what to watch for."

"Is she well?" Any sane woman would walk away now. But I was not ordinary. I had access to things, events, reports of UFOs and other phenomena the everyday citizen had never seen. Believing aliens were real was no stretch for me. Accepting that

Kassius had traveled here from another solar system to find me? *Me?* Well, *that* was the crazy bit.

"She is healthy and whole, living with Alexius on Arturri."

"Show me the scar." I blurted the order before I could think better of it. On our second mission I'd seen my Kass, the Kass in the game, without his shirt on. *That* Kassius had a jagged circular scar on the back of his left shoulder. Wide lines. Bigger than my hand. Old.

No actor could fake that.

"With pleasure." His grin as he stepped back was not what I had expected, and the air caught in my lungs as I watched him pull the black shirt over his head. His chest was... massive. Muscled. Perfect. But a lot of men had nice physiques. Wide shoulders. Arms rippling with strength.

I'd been staring too long, and he seemed content to allow it. "Turn around," I ordered.

He did so, slowly. When he faced away from me, I stepped forward with a gasp. The scar was there. Old. Healed. A mark of extreme pain. Exactly as I remembered. "Oh my God." Fingers trembling, I traced the mark with a quiet sigh. "You're real."

"I am."

"How did you get this?"

"That is a story for another day." He rotated and I couldn't bear to stop touching him as my palm slid from back to shoulder to chest. I didn't want to give him up. Not yet.

"I actually believe you." I reached up, cupped his square jaw, touched his lips—with something other than my mouth—for the first time. "You really are Kass."

He stroked my hair back, watched his fingers as he ran them through it. "I am. You chose me in your beginning assessment. We have worked together all this time to get through the training."

"Hold that thought." I stepped away from his touch and pulled my cell phone from my jacket pocket. I had to let Lily know what was happening. If I disappeared, too, poor Lily would freak. What if she got scared or distracted or depressed and didn't finish the game? What if Darius never came for her and she died not knowing what had happened to us. No. Not okay.

I pulled up her contact info, grateful we'd exchanged numbers, and my fingers flew over the small digital keyboard.

Lily, it's Mia. The game is real. Jamie is on Velerion with Alexius. I'm leaving now with Kass. Finish the game. Darius will come for you.

I hit send and waited as Kass patiently watched me. Less than thirty seconds later I received Lily's response.

WTF? Is this a joke? What??????

I was grinning now, bubbling over with anticipation and excitement and happiness. My life was about to go in a completely new direction, and I was so ready. So damn ready to do something different.

Not a joke. Finish the game. Darius will come. See you on Velerion.

I turned off my phone and slipped it back into the jacket pocket. I was about to jump all over Kassius Remeas, and I didn't need my phone's camera or microphone on to capture the moment. "What now?" I moved toward him and placed my palms flat on his chest. He was warm and strong and looking at me like I was his favorite thing in the universe. All things which made him impossible to resist, even if I'd wanted to. Which I didn't.

"You cannot imagine how I've longed for you." He traced my lower lip with his thumb as I took a deep breath, learning his scent for the first time.

My imagination was pretty spectacular, so he was wrong there.

"I don't want to wait any longer. I can't." He

rolled his hips into me, and I felt why. "Mia, please say you've been as crazy as me for this moment."

I didn't want to wait either. God, I soooo didn't. "Yes, I've been crazy. God, the things I thought about you."

His jaw clenched. "I want to hear them all. Later."

I licked my lips, gave a little nod. I'd never been so aroused, so eager for a man. We'd only kissed and God, we'd just met. But I *knew* Kass. Needed him.

"Don't wait," I told him, running my hands over him because... because *he was mine.* "Please. I want you, too."

A deep growl emanated from his chest, and then he moved. My shirt was pushed up over my breasts, and his mouth latched on to my nipple. He gave one hard suck but growled again, this time in frustration a second before he tugged my bra cup down. "Fuck, all mine."

He took me back in his mouth and sucked. Hard. It reached my core and I moaned, suddenly feeling empty and achy and desperate for more.

He lifted his head, and I looked into his dark eyes. "That sound is for me alone. No one on the other side of that door will have such a reward."

I nodded, tangled my fingers in his hair. "Kass. More."

He worked at my pants as I toed off my heels, flinging them across the room. When he couldn't figure out that the zipper was on the side, I pushed his hands away and worked it down on my own. Kass did his pants, and I stilled when his hard length sprang free.

"*Scheisse.*" I'd had good sex before, but I had a feeling the reason I hadn't been fully satisfied was because of what was in front of me. Alien cock. Kass was big and his body was more than proportional. He was thick and long like a porn star with a broad crown that made me wonder if I could get that monster in my mouth.

My body clenched in anticipation, but I knew I'd be feeling him for days. It would be a reminder of exactly how real he was.

"My pants are down, bond mate. You don't need to praise me." He gripped the base and stroked it from root to tip. Once. Twice. A bead of pre-cum oozed from the slit.

"You're cocky."

His dark brow winged up and he grinned. "In so many ways. You wet for me?"

I stepped on my pants, pushing them down the

rest of the way, and shucked them off with a flick of my foot. I'd taken my panties with them, so I was bare except for my shirt up over my breasts and my pushed-down bra.

Reaching out, I took his hand and brought it between my thighs. When he slipped two fingers inside, I went up on my toes, gripped his taut forearms.

"Don't make me wait any longer," I said.

He didn't. He pulled his hand away, slid it around my hip to cup my ass. He had me lifted and my legs wrapped around his waist in under a second, his cock at my entrance, and then he lowered me down.

I arched my back at the stretch, but my need for him eased the way.

He gave me a second to adjust, and our gazes met. Held. I nodded and then he moved. This wasn't gentle. Or sweet. It was true fucking. Wall pounding, deep thrusts that had him filling me completely. Over and over. Hard. Our bodies slapped together, and his fingers dug into my ass.

I didn't want it any other way. I was frantic for him, and the way he moved without any kind of rhythm, almost desperate in finding his pleasure in me, said he was frantic as well.

I needed this. I needed him. No one else would

do. The craving I had built up for him could only be soothed through this rough coupling. "Kass," I whimpered, dropping my head back against the wall.

His repeated chants of *mine* were all he said.

My clit was worked with every roll of his hips, and I came hard, biting my lip.

Kass followed right behind me, his ragged growl in my ear as he leaned in and filled me with his cum, with every bit of how badly he'd wanted me.

This was insane. We were sweaty. Out of breath. I was going to have bruises down my spine, and my body had taken a pummeling. But there was no question in my mind—and in my body—that Kass was real.

And as soon as we pulled ourselves back together, I was going with him. To another planet. Another life.

To Velerion.

*S*tarfighter *MCS Kassius Remeas,* Battleship Resolution, *Landing Bay*

I SET the speed of the shuttle to its maximum and was in the *Resolution's* landing bay within minutes of coming through the jump gate and back into the Vega System. I was home. Even better, Mia sat next to me, where she would be from now on, her face calmer than I expected as she took in the stars, the planet below us, and the giant battleship we would call home. Autopiloting features kicked in and pulled us inside before settling our small shuttle into one of the specialty berths.

"Welcome to the *Resolution,* Starfighters."

Mia gasped at the greeting that filled the cockpit and I grinned. "Thank you, *Resolution.* Please notify General Jennix of our arrival."

"Already done, sir."

A battleship comms officer had just called me *sir.* I grinned. Yes. I could get used to that.

Mia was rubbing her head again, and I wanted to pull her into my arms and take her pain away. "How are you? I can delay if you need more time to adjust to the cipher implant." I'd shared the details of the implant injection and the side effects and offered her a sedative so she could sleep through the worst of it. She had, of course, declined.

"I'll be fine. I've had worse. And I don't want to miss anything."

"Of course not." Not my Mia. She wanted to see everything. Analyze our surroundings. Take in every detail. Already her gaze scanned what little was visible of the *Battleship Resolution's* landing bay. She turned her head to look outside of the shuttle, and I barely resisted the urge to stroke the soft skin of her neck. Again.

The dark swirling mark below her ear made me want to strut around with this beautiful, talented female and show her off. Let everyone see the marks on her neck and mine, the marks of a pair-bonded

Starfighter team. But the cipher implant was busy working on Mia's neural network, the cipher's micro-electric nanites connecting with her human nervous system to make sure she could understand every-thing she saw and heard out here in space. Once fully integrated, they would help her see more clearly, increase her reaction times, and help her integrate with Velerion ships' systems at maximum efficiency.

Didn't mean the damn implants were without issues. The dagger-to-the-skull levels of pain as they duplicated, then merged with the host's neurons was not pleasant. And the deep lines of pain around Mia's eyes and mouth had not lessened much during our trip back to the Vega System.

"Are you sure, Mia? I'm sorry for implanting it, but there was no choice. I can take you to medical. I can also offer you something for the pain."

"No. Kass, I'm fine."

No, she was not. But she was a fully trained Starfighter MCS. Deadly. Sexy. And mine. If she said she was all right, I would honor her wishes. And watch over her whether she liked the attention or not. I inspected Mia in her Starfighter MCS uniform and allowed the sense of pride, contentment, and lust to wash over me. She was mine. She was magnificent. And she was really here. After packing a few of her things, inspecting the small but comfortable place she lived, giving her pleasure until we both passed out from exhaustion, then a few hours of rest, I'd escorted her to my ship. When I'd arrived on Earth, I landed my shuttle while the humans were sleeping, using the autopilot feature to park my vessel at the bottom of the city's large river once I'd disembarked. Even without the water, my ship would have remained hidden from Earth's sensors by advanced stealth technology.

To return, I'd walked her to the river's edge in the dead of night and summoned the shuttle. Watching her face as the ship appeared out of thin air had been the most fun I'd had in years. I'd felt like a little boy showing off a new favorite toy.

There was no question then of Mia wondering if it was only a game.

Several hours of flying, one trip through the jump gate, and we had arrived.

"We're home, Mia. Welcome to Velerion. Well, to the Velerion *Battleship Resolution,* currently under the command of General Jennix."

"Holy shit." Mia stood and followed as I led the way to the shuttle's hatch. She glanced around before stepping out onto the ramp. "This is *Battlestar*

Galactica, next-level, *Star Wars* insane." She reached out and ran her fingers through my hair, which was quickly becoming one of my favorite things in life. "Do you guys have *the Force?*"

"What is the force?"

She was smiling wider than I'd ever seen. "You know, mind control and telekinesis and knowing things about the future, or sensing when someone you care about is in trouble. Telepathy, I guess."

Interesting. "No. Do humans have these powers?"

She shook her head. "Only in movies." She placed her palm over the mark on her neck and winked at me. "So far, anyway. We'll see what these crazy implants do to us."

She had a point. She was the second human to have received them. Our scientists assured us they were safe for all species, but that didn't mean they had a clue what the cipher technology would do to humans.

When I walked down the shuttle's back ramp, Mia's hand in mine, there—fuck—stood Captain Sponder, blocking our way.

"Captain." I shifted Mia behind me, putting my bulk between Sponder and my bonded one. I waited for the verbal explosion I knew was coming. Sponder wasn't supposed to be here. He was normally on the surface of Velerion, inside Eos Station, strutting around like he owned the place. Why was he on the battleship?

"Shuttle Pilot, what the hell is this bullshit that you've been pair bonded and promoted to Starfighter MCS? You were never approved for the training program."

"Actually I was," I countered. Mia was proof of that.

"Who approved your training?"

I grinned. I couldn't stop myself. "You did."

"I'll have your head this time, Pilot," he snapped. The veins in his temples pulsed.

The fucker wasn't just a nemesis who wanted to see me kept down, but now he was following me around? Haunting me like a ghost? He was old enough to be my father and had the attitude and personality of a Velerion jungle rat. He hated me.

The feeling was mutual. He was known for harassing lower-ranking staff, especially females. I had hacked the system to transfer one of his favorite targets to serve under a different leader. I'd denied him his fun and games, his torment of someone weaker and vulnerable.

He'd suspected what I'd done, but I never shared the video with him. He had no proof. Sure, I'd just admitted it, but again, no real proof. The silent standoff had lasted for more than a year until he'd refused to give me clearance to enter Starfighter training. That was why I'd hacked into the system and given it to myself. I'd taken my career into my own hands because I knew he'd never let me out from under this thumb. I knew too much but probably not everything. I was a threat to his career.

And now I outranked him.

He was not happy. I'd pulled off the ultimate deception right under his nose. I'd gone around the one and only blockade he'd erected that had kept me from becoming a Starfighter. He knew, but he couldn't prove anything. Again.

"Are you threatening a superior officer?" I asked.

"I'll speak to the general about this." Sponder's hair was gray. His face was lined. His eyes were almost black and void of any kind of compassion or warmth. I had to wonder if he wasn't part cyborg with the lack of emotion and empathy he routinely displayed.

"I believe my rank is now Starfighter MCS," I replied, my voice deepening. He wasn't going to temper my happiness. Mia had remained silent through all this, and he was wasting my time and ruining her arrival.

I squeezed Mia's hand and moved to skirt around him, but he held up his hand in front of my chest. I bristled because of my pair bond. He could fuck with me all he wanted, but he wouldn't even *look* at Mia.

"You were not approved for the training program."

I stood beside him, but we faced opposite directions. "Yes. I was."

"No, you certainly were not."

It seemed we were going to argue in circles.

I turned to face him, tucking Mia behind me. I hadn't realized how pointed his nose was. "Because you made sure of it."

He tipped his head. "That's right. The Starfighter program doesn't need anyone like you."

I smiled then, in victory. "Actually they do."

"I will write you up for interfering with the training protocols and deny your transfer to the Starfighter program."

"You may file a complaint with General Jennix, Captain, if you feel you have been wronged by a higher-ranking officer. If you will excuse me, I have my pair bond to orient to our new home."

Sponder leaned to look around me, as if he hadn't even noticed Mia was with me before. He lowered his hand and practically snarled his response. "You are not my superior, Pilot. I'll see to that. And this female, wherever you found her, can go back under whatever rock you two crawled from."

"Are you threatening her?" I growled. He was gravely mistaken if he intended to interfere. Nothing would stop me from claiming what I'd worked so hard to achieve. Not with Mia's life on the line as well. Her future. Her career. When it had only been my future at stake, I had put up with his bullshit, worked my way around him. But Mia was expecting me to be there for her, fighting beside her.

Mia would need me. To pilot the *Phantom,* to have her back, to help her hack into Dark Fleet networks, to keep her safe and happy and thoroughly pleasured. She'd matched herself to me, *chosen me* through the complex questionnaire program that ultimately united us as a connected, highly specialized fighting team. We were a bonded fighting pair. We had completed every mission in the Starfighter Training Academy. Together.

I admired her, had fought beside her for months, and, if I were being brutally honest, I'd already fallen in love with her. Her determination. Her brilliant mind. Her sassy mouth.

She was beside me now, and *nothing* would break

us apart. Not only did Velerion law prevent anything from severing a pair bond, but I would see to it that nothing separated us.

A communications tech approached. He saluted Mia first, then me, then tipped his head to Sponder almost as an afterthought. "Starfighter MCS. Welcome aboard. We've been expecting you."

I glanced at Mia, who looked a little over-whelmed but happy. I was pleased by his words. *Starfighter MCS*. Yeah, that sounded perfect.

"His rank is lieutenant, and he is nothing more than a shuttle pilot," Sponder snapped at the tech, whose spine stiffened. That was how the asshole had always expected me to respond to him, but I'd always refused. I didn't kowtow to assholes like him.

The tech looked between the three of us, unsure. Then he stiffened to attention as a tall woman approached. "General Jennix," the tech said. "This is our new Starfighter MCS bonded pair. Kassius Remeas of Velerion and Mia Becker of Earth."

The general smiled and practically rubbed her hands together in subdued glee. "Welcome aboard, Starfighters. I am General Jennix, and you have been placed under my command. You answer directly to me and only to me." She emphasized the last as she stared down Captain Sponder.

I nodded at her, pleased the general had confirmed that our new roles were secure. "Thank you, General."

"Graves will show you to your new quarters. While I'm sure you would like to take some time to learn about your new home, I need you both in my office within the hour. We have a situation." She smiled in direct contrast to the chill that raced down my spine at her words. "Starfighter Pilots Jamie and Alex intercepted another IPBM less than three hours ago. I apologize, Mia Becker, but you are not going to get a chance to rest."

Mia had remained silent up to this point, and I wondered exactly what she was thinking. It was not like her to hold her tongue. At least she had never minced words during training. But she was on a battleship. In space. There was nothing here remotely similar to Earth. I could imagine how overwhelmed she was. The only familiar thing was me.

"Thank you, General," she murmured. "I don't sleep much anyway."

Mia's words made the general chuckle. "Very good. Congratulations on completing the Starfighter Training Academy. You are the second from Earth to do so."

"Starfighter Jamie Miller and I are friends. We trained together."

The general nodded. "Excellent." She looked to me. "We are eager for you both to join us."

Meaning she didn't give a shit about Sponder. She wanted Starfighter MCSs and now.

"Thank you, General," I said, offering her a respectful nod.

"Lieutenant Remeas's transfer to Starfighter MCS is denied, General," Sponder snapped, moving to stand at my shoulder. "I think you should know that this shuttle pilot hacked into the training program and entered himself into the system against my direct orders."

"Captain Sponder, I assume," Jennix replied. While she was shorter than Sponder, she looked down her nose at him. Her clipped words and steely stare indicated she was not impressed by my previous superior.

Sponder dipped his chin, although I doubted he had a deferential bone in his body.

The general opened her mouth to respond, but Mia beat her to it. "If he hacked your security, Captain, that is more proof of exactly how talented an MCS he will be. Either that or you badly need a lesson in security protocols."

"No, sir." Sponder might challenge me but even he wasn't stupid enough to disrespect or disobey an unknown Starfighter MCS in front of General Jennix. He was a spiteful, bitter man, but he was not suicidal.

"Both excellent points, Starfighter," Jennix agreed as she returned her attention to Sponder. "I'll send an audit team to Eos Station first thing tomorrow to review those protocols."

"Yes, General. Thank you."

I bit back a laugh. Mia had basically just blamed my hacking on Sponder *and* made known that he was at fault for having lax security. And now he would have to deal with the bureaucrats. Velerion auditors would pick apart his entire system, interview everyone under his command, rewrite his programs, and reorganize his access controls. Sponder was going to be in a living hell for weeks.

Captain Sponder's security was excellent. Hacking the system had taken concentrated effort over a span of days. His system was top-notch. I was better.

"Starfighter Kassius Remeas is required to report for duty immediately," General Jennix advised, then looked at me. "In fact, I need you to confirm acceptance of the pair bond now so I can transfer control of the *Phantom* immediately."

Mia looked confused. "The *Phantom?*"

"Of course. That is the name of your ship, is it not?" Jennix asked even as she shoved a tablet toward me.

The smooth screen split to show one half with my face and the other half of the screen displayed what looked like part of the training program. Mia's avatar and her training stats were listed as well as the fact that the training had been completed, she'd graduated, accepted the role as MCS, and accepted the pair bond with me.

My stomach dropped as if I'd been sucker punched. Mia had said yes—obviously, since she was here. I'd known she was mine, but seeing it on the screen? Her acceptance sent me reeling. All that was required was my final confirmation. I placed my palm on the screen, and certainty settled over me. This was real. Final. No one could take Mia or the Starfighter rank from me. Ever.

Sponder snatched the tablet away. "General, I beg of you. Please listen. This recruit entered the training program without approval. He should be in the brig, not promoted to Starfighter MCS."

I smirked as Sponder continued his ill-advised rant.

"I will return to Velerion, to Eos Station with the pilot and take care of him for you," he continued. "He will be demoted for his blatant disregard of a direct order as well as a long list of other infractions."

Other infractions? I refrained from rolling my eyes, but it took an act of will. No doubt this "long list" would be created on the shuttle ride from *Battleship Resolution* back to the surface.

I wanted to punch the asshole in the face, but doing so in front of General Jennix wouldn't be a smart move.

"How he entered the system is irrelevant," Jennix said, and I inwardly sighed in relief. "We need Starfighters now. You're aware of the current state of affairs with the Dark Fleet. The IPBMs and where they are made needs to be discovered immediately. We need fighters like Kassius and Mia or Velerion as we know it will not survive. Captain Sponder, Starfighter Kassius Remeas is no longer under your command. I expect you to return to the surface, to Eos Station, and await further orders."

"Yes, sir," Sponder grumbled, recognizing he could do no more.

She looked at me and then Mia. "Starfighters, my office within the hour. Graves?"

The tech who had originally greeted us stepped forward. "Yes, General."

"Show them to their quarters. I've had enough bullshit for one morning." Jennix left without another word, and an awkward silence descended.

Mia tilted her head to inspect Sponder from head to toe. It was disappointing that he was the first one she'd met here. "Well, that didn't go well for you, did it?"

Sponder stiffened and turned on his heel.

I pursed my lips to stifle a smile. "Enjoy the audit, *Captain*," I called.

He halted in his tracks for a count of three, refused to face me, and walked away so stiffly I was sure he would compress carbon into a diamond between his ass cheeks.

With a grin, I saluted Sponder's retreating back for the final time. The action held no respect. I wasn't going to miss that face, but I had a feeling this wasn't over between us. It didn't matter. I didn't need to be his friend. Hell, I didn't even care if I was his enemy. I had what I wanted because *I'd* made it happen. I had won.

"You hacked into the system to be added as a Starfighter candidate?" Mia murmured.

"Oh yes."

"Huh. I guess you're good at computers."

"Not as good as you are."

The compliment made her smile, which made me want to kiss her. But then I always wanted to kiss her. Among other things.

"If you would come with me, Starfighters, I will show you where your quarters are, then lead you to the general's office." The tech was a saint. He had watched the byplay between all of us with a carefully blank expression.

"You work directly with the general?" I asked as we followed him down a series of halls. I allowed all thoughts of Sponder to disappear.

"I am her personal emissary. Lieutenant Graves, at your service, sirs."

"Thank you, Graves," Mia said.

Graves lifted a brow at me. "You made an enemy today, sir."

I shrugged. "It wasn't today."

"Assholes don't make good friends anyway," Mia commented.

I lifted her hand to my lips and placed a kiss on

the back of it. "As always, my Mia, you speak the truth."

"Indeed." Graves's face resumed its blank expression as he led us out of the landing bay to start our future. Based on the haste of the general, it was going to be action-packed.

 *ia*

ALL I SAW of the battleship was Graves's back and lots and lots of corridors. To say that I felt as if I'd stepped into a sci-fi movie was an understatement. I *felt* like I was on a battleship. It was massive. I'd need a GPS and a compass to work my way around, and we'd only switched floors twice.

People—Velerions and others most likely in the Galactic Alliance—passed and nodded their heads respectfully. I felt as if they were eyeing me funny, but I had on the same uniform they did. Well, except theirs didn't have exactly the same Starfighter emblem. When I'd first put the new uniform on, I'd felt like I was dressing up for Halloween. I'd twisted my hair into a knot and slid my feet into the pair of boots exactly like the ones my character wore in the game. Except this was real. The fabric was soft but strong. Apparently both fire- and bulletproof, at least partially.

I would have refused to wear it, but Kass sported the same clothing, both of us in fresh uniforms he'd had ready on board his shuttle. A matching date costume then. But when we'd descended the ramp and ran into that jerk Sponder, it had all become real.

We'd barely stepped foot into our new quarters, which looked like an expensive suite in a five-star hotel. Really posh living quarters for soldiers. When I asked Graves about it, he'd shrugged.

"Starfighters are rare. Special. We take care of them the best we can."

I didn't have time to explore, but the rooms Kass and I would, apparently, be living in from now on were luxurious, far better than my apartment in Berlin. And we were in space. On a battleship, for God's sake.

"How many Starfighter pairs are on this ship?" I asked.

Graves didn't hesitate. "Two pilot pair bonds and the two of you."

"Three?"

"Yes. After the Starfighter base attack last year, the pilots were shared strategically. You are the first and only Starfighter MCS pair we have."

"On the ship?"

"In the Velerion fleet."

Oh shit.

"Your arrival is fortuitous. The general is anxious to task you with discovering the source of the new attacks. With no MCS team, we have been unable to track Queen Raya's forces or pinpoint the location of their production facilities."

Kass walked through the rooms as I spoke to Graves. "They'll bring our belongings?"

Graves nodded. "Your personal items have been removed from Eos Station and will arrive shortly. Starfighter Mia Becker, your items will be off-loaded from the shuttle and delivered before you are done with the general."

"Very well. Let's go talk to the general."

Graves led the way through another maze of corridors and down two more floors to Jennix's office. He hadn't spoken more, thankfully. I would have been overwhelmed if he'd given us a running commentary. I was aware Kass was new to this assignment as well, but I had no idea if he'd ever been on this ship before or if he was mapping in his head as I was.

The entire time he was at my side. Holding my hand. Watching me. I hadn't missed how he'd blocked Sponder's access to me, but I didn't need protection from a guy like him. I worked in the law enforcement and intelligence communities. Assholes didn't exist solely in space. Even then, better to deal with an asshole than an evil monster. We had those on Earth, too.

I kept firm control of my mind, refusing to allow my tendency to overanalyze everything to take over. The ship, the crew, the reality we faced was a lot to absorb. This wasn't Germany. This wasn't Earth. This wasn't even Velerion. We were on a battleship floating in outer space!

"Starfighters, General," Graves said as we entered her office, then disappeared to tackle some other duty.

"Mia!"

Before I could even nod to my new commanding officer, I was wrapped in a huge hug.

"Oh my God, I can't believe you're here! Isn't it crazy we had to meet in space instead of on Earth?

We were supposed to take this meeting via comms, but I refused. I *had* to meet you in person. I mean, it *is* crazy but—"

"Let your friend breathe, bonded one," a voice gently chided.

I was pushed back, and I could now see more of the hugger than just her brown hair. It was the voice that was familiar first, but then the face. Or it was the avatar of her I knew.

"Jamie?" I wondered, eyeing my long-lost friend up and down.

She had dark hair, a round face, and a huge smile. Bouncing on the balls of her feet, she could barely contain herself.

"Yes! Can you believe it?"

I looked to the man beside her. I recognized him from the game as well. "Wow," I said, letting my brain catch up. "You're Alexius."

He nodded and grinned. "I have heard much about you from Jamie these past few days. You look just like in the training program. I'm eager for combat with you. Your MCS skills are brilliant." Alex turned to Kass. "Another pleasure. We are lucky Velerions to have these women as our pair bonds."

Kass set his hand on my shoulder. "Agreed."

Jamie took my hand and tugged me to a chair. "I watched as you beat the game," she said.

I remembered the feeling when I won, when Lily was shouting in my ear. As I wondered where Jamie was—and it turned out she'd been watching all along. "I didn't know where you went. I looked everywhere for you."

She looked sheepish. "Except space."

I nodded. "Except space. Why couldn't you have left a note?"

"And say what?" she asked, arching a dark brow. "The game is real and I'm going to Velerion with Alex?"

"Yes. I texted Lily so she wouldn't worry when I disappeared, too. Also to let her know Darius was going to come knocking."

Jamie laughed. "Oh man, I wish I could see that. Lily is going to totally freak."

"What are you doing here on the battleship? Kass said you were on some moon base and the general mentioned you'd intercepted a bomb of some kind."

"You know about the IPBMs?"

I nodded. "Well, I didn't know what they were called, but the last training mission in the game changed and included a ship loaded with bombs that could destroy an entire planet. I thought it was in-game, science-fiction bullshit."

"They're real."

"Great."

She frowned. "They're no fun. But I don't have to tell you they're real. It took me a while to grasp that *everything* up here is real. Everything we encountered in the game is real. Every moon base and asteroid and planet out here. It's like living in the game. I even got to meet Queen Raya, personally."

I stared at her. She'd met Queen Raya? *Scheisse.* "*And?*"

"Psycho bitch, per the usual crazed, power-hungry megalomaniac."

"Does she look the same as well?"

"Right down to the dramatic, dark gray trench coat."

"Well, it won't be too much of a leap for me. I believed it was real when Kass showed up."

"When I showed you my scar," Kass added. "And other parts of my body."

He winked.

I blushed.

Jamie grinned.

Alex leaned in and said something to Kass I

couldn't hear, although if the smile on his face was any indication, he was amused.

I pursed my lips in fake annoyance, but I wasn't embarrassed. The way Alex was looking at Jamie indicated their relationship was as hot as mine with Kass. And they'd been together two weeks longer.

If Kass and I had sex within ten minutes of meeting, we could have too many orgasms to count by day fourteen. My body was still sore from the hard ride Kass had given me at work. And at my apartment. In my shower. On my couch.

On Earth. God, that seemed so far away.

"You never answered my question. Why are you here? On the *Resolution*, I mean."

Jamie looked up at Alex. "We completed our shift on IPBM watch, and we heard through comms about the new Starfighter MCS."

I took her hand, gave it a squeeze. "It's good to see you. To meet you. Here. God, this is insane," I said, my heart pounding. It was exhilarating. I was able to share this with one of my best friends.

"How's Lily?" she asked. "I'm sure she will win soon and join us."

"Yes, but she's worried about you. And now me probably as well."

"But you said you texted her. What did you say?"

"I told her to beat the game, that Velerion was real, that you were already here, and I was leaving Earth with Kass." My smile grew. "And I told her Darius was going to come for her."

"The sooner she finishes, the sooner—"

"We can have another Starfighter Titan team on the ground. We need Titan units to protect our infantry and pound the enemy into dust," Jennix finished, coming into the room. I turned at her voice. "Just like we need more Starfighter MCS teams and Starfighter Pilots. Welcome to Velerion, Starfighter Becker."

I was pretty darn sure that wasn't *exactly* where Jamie was going with her statement, but we shared a grin. We both knew what happened when a smoking-hot fighter from Velerion showed up on a girl's doorstep.

Jamie stood. I mimicked her. Kass was at my side, and Alex moved to flank Jamie.

The general glanced between us. "I am pleased that you have had a reunion," she commented, walked around her desk, and sat. I only sat once the others did, unsure of protocol. "But that's going to have to wait. I'm sure Starfighter Miller told you about how they intercepted the latest IPBM aimed at Velerion."

Kass nodded and so did I. We didn't have details, but I knew enough.

"Starfighters, please catch the others up on what's happened lately."

Alex began. "During our escape from Queen Raya's base on Syrax, the queen deployed a new weapon. We discovered she has IPBMs, interplanetary ballistic missiles, powerful enough to blow up Velerion."

"Or Earth," Jamie added. The grim look on her face told me there was more to this story.

Alex continued. "The two IPBM launches that day were destroyed. Since then we've had Starfighters in the air around the clock to ensure when the queen uses another, we destroy them before they reach their target."

"Has she?" I asked.

"Three," the general added.

We turned to face her. "Starfighters Jamie and Alex will return to Arturri for their standard sleep requirement. In the meantime you two will head to a heavily traveled trading route, in stealth mode. We have multiple reports of Dark Fleet ships moving from outside the system to Xandrax."

I must have looked confused, because the general clarified.

"The Dark Fleet and its most powerful members are not from our system. Queen Raya's involvement with them is relatively new, as is their support for her attempt to conquer Velerion. They would love to have this system under their control and Queen Raya is playing a very dangerous game in choosing to deal with them. The IPBM technology was banned by the Galactic Alliance treaties centuries ago and should the Alliance systems decide to get involved, our war could expand to include multiple galaxies and hundreds of star systems. The Galactic Alliance does not want that to happen."

Wait, what? That wasn't in the game. "So how did Queen Raya get her hands on the IPSMs?"

"We know she is in league with the Dark Fleet. But as to how the weapons actually arrived in our system and where she is hiding them? That's what we need to know. The Dark Fleet is quick to send ships and spies, but they do not normally risk war with the Galactic Alliance. We could be dealing with an independent party, or the Dark Fleet could be testing the Alliance's willingness to go to war over two small planets."

So, arms dealers in space. Pissing contests. Politics. Posturing. Sheesh. People were people and war was war and there were asshole bad guys in space, too. Hopefully I could do my job right this time and not get anyone else killed. Or an entire planet of anyones.

I was going to vomit on my nice, new boots right here in the general's office. Damn it.

"You will attach yourselves to one of the Dark Fleet ships and hack into the ship's comm and data networks to discover the location of the IPBM stockpile and, if possible, the location of their production facility. If we can destroy those locations, we can put the Starfighters back onto regular mission rotations. We've been playing defense these past weeks. It's time to turn the tables."

Jamie yawned. I was about to crawl out of my skin, and Jamie was drooping, leaning into Alex like it was nap time and he was her favorite pillow. I could relate.

"Dismissed, Starfighters. Excellent work today."

Jamie stood, then gave me a brilliant smile. I raised my hand for a high five. It was something we were able to do in the game to congratulate each other, and it was the first time we'd been able to do it in real life.

"See you soon," she said.

"Count on it," I replied.

Alex bowed to the general, then nodded to me and Kass before he took Jamie's hand as they left.

"Here are the details of the mission," the general said, then shared them. I paid close attention as I had during the pre-game sequence. But this wasn't a game. By the time she was finished, I was ready to get in the real *Phantom*.

"Show us what you've got, Starfighters," she finished.

"We'll find out where they've got those missiles, General," I said.

"In stealth mode, please," she replied. "I do not want to lose you two on your first mission."

I looked to Kass and he nodded. Yeah, we were going to steal everything the general needed from the Dark Fleet, and they wouldn't even know we were there.

6

assius

LIEUTENANT GRAVES ESCORTED us from General Jennix's office to the launch bay that served the Starfighter teams aboard the *Battleship Resolution*. Our first stop was the mission prep area, where we were brought our flight suits. Graves waited while Mia and I changed from our standard black uniform into the sleek Starfighter space suit. The material was thin and comfortable, but I knew the suit would protect us from small laser blasts, was fireproof and, with the retractable helmet all Velerion space suits had stored in the collar, capable of keeping us alive on a spacewalk, if necessary. The uniform looked almost exactly like the standard Starfighter uniform, except the space suits had the integrated helmet and the swirl on the chest was silver, not black.

Once we were in our flight gear, Graves walked us through the small launch area. There were two Starfighter Pilot teams serving on the *Resolution,* and their sleek fighting ships shone with a glowing metallic black that made me think of danger and war and death. Their larger ships were meant for combat, loaded with weapons and fuel. The MCS ships would be just as fast but smaller. Sleeker. With limited weapons and most of the interior loaded with communication and computing equipment rather than cannons.

I was guessing, of course. I'd never seen one, only in the training simulation I'd completed with Mia. The stealthy MCS ships were so secretive that no one but the Starfighter specific mechanics' teams were allowed anywhere near them. And that was only with permission from the Starfighter assigned to the ship. As the pilot and secondary MCS officer, I was there to serve in a support role for Mia. Make sure she arrived safely, evaded enemies and survived to fight another day.

Although I was the pilot, The *Phantom* was Mia's ship, not mine. Her position as the lead MCS officer on our team meant the ship belonged to her, as I did. Body and soul. I wished for more time alone with her. To get to know her. Inside her head. Inside her body. That would have to wait... for now. I wasn't sure if I could hold off long. I wanted to touch her. Watch her as I made her pliant, as I made her scream.

Mia had a spring in her step.

"Headache gone?"

She grinned at me. "Mostly. I can't believe I'm going to see the *Phantom*. For real."

Her excitement was contagious, and I grinned back as we increased our pace, causing Graves to lift a brow as he hustled to remain a step ahead of us.

I thought I was mentally prepared to meet my future head-on. However, when I saw the *Phantom* for the first time, my entire body went taut with a feeling of dread... and elation. The ship was a living, breathing nightmare to my senses. It was darker than deep space. Staring at the outline of the hull, I squinted as the edges blurred, moved, and reappeared in a state of constant change. Like a river of black water flowing along its banks. At night. A highly advanced network of contrasting panels made the outer hull literally shimmer like a gloomy mirage, despite the fact that Mia and I stood less than ten paces away.

This was a ship that dealt in secrets. Shadows.

Death. And I'd hacked into the systems to be here.

"Oh my God." Mia seemed hypnotized by *Phantom*, her whispered words sending a chill from the base of my skull to my chest. She recognized the importance of this moment as much as I. She'd worked hard to be here. Not just in the training program but in her life skills, her Earth job. She was brilliant, and it would pay off while we were fighting the Dark Fleet.

Graves motioned the two mechanics in the area over to us. One male, one female, they appeared to be young but walked with confidence. "Starfighters Mia and Kassius, meet your pair-bonded mechs, Vintis and Arria. Mechs, meet our newest Starfighter MCS bonded pair, Mia Becker of Earth and Kassius Remeas, former shuttle pilot at Eos Station."

The two looked like twins in their dark blue uniforms, the silver Starfighter insignia swirling bright on each of their chests.

Mia held out her hand, thumb pointed toward the ceiling. "I'm Mia. Nice to meet you."

The two stared at her offered hand for a few seconds, confused. Finally Arria held out her hand in turn. Mia grabbed Arria's hand, squeezed, and lifted her hand up, then pulled it down several times before releasing her.

"It's an honor, Starfighters." Arria's wide smile held no hint of deception while she studied Mia as if looking at a goddess in the flesh. I was awestruck, so it was no wonder others were too. As long as I was the one taking her to my bed, I would share.

Done staring, Arria turned to me and touched two fingers to her temple in a standard Velerion salute. I responded in kind as Mia grabbed Vintis's hand and followed the same odd sequence of events with the much larger male.

"Vintis," she said by way of greeting.

"Proud to be part of your team, Starfighter."

"As am I. We will keep your ship in perfect shape, sirs," Arria assured us. "Vintis handles the heavy lifting, and I squeeze into the tight spaces. We're the best mechs on the *Resolution.*"

Vintis scoffed. "Best on Velerion."

I liked their attitude.

Graves took the opportunity to clear his throat. I had completely forgotten he was there. "Buy your new mechs a drink when you return alive from your mission, Starfighters. The target vessel will be passing through Velerion space in a few hours. You need to move."

Vintis looked disappointed but knew his job. "You're ready to go. Fuel and power backups are at full capacity. Weapons loaded and armed. The entire system has been inspected three times over since we got her on board. The *Phantom* is ready to fly."

Mia glanced over her shoulder at me, her eyes glowing with excitement. "Kass?"

I wanted to grab her, kiss her, make her whimper with need.

So I did.

Grabbing her upper arms, I tugged her close, fused my mouth to hers. She was surprised for a split second, then opened for me. Our tongues tangled, heads slanted to take the kiss deeper. More. *More.* My cock throbbed with the need for more.

Instead I pulled back. Grinned when she blinked her eyes open.

"This is it, my pair bond. Let's go."

Mia licked her lips and I groaned. She left me behind to run her hand over the outer shell of our ship as she made her way to the ramp. "She's beautiful. I can't believe this is real. It's like I'm in an episode of *Star Trek* or something. No red shirt, either."

I had no idea what she was talking about, but after I adjusted my cock so it was more comfortable in my uniform pants, I led the way inside. "Let us begin our trek to the stars, my Mia."

"Glad you hacked your way here?" she asked.

I grinned. "Hell, yeah."

With a leap covering the final few steps, Mia smashed her hand down on the portal controls to retract the ramp and close the doors. I wondered for a second how she knew to do that, then realized we'd both watched this sequence of events hundreds of times in the training program. She walked inside and craned her neck, looked in every direction.

"This is exactly like the game. Even the flat bolts on the floor paneling. This is unreal."

I grabbed her hips, pulled her close for a quick kiss, and forced myself to step back. "I can't wait to fly her. Come on."

We jogged to the cockpit, which took all of ten steps, and I slipped into the pilot's seat as she took up position in the copilot's chair. Once we reached our target, her seat would slide into the direction facing opposite mine where she would have access to a large array of surveillance and hacking equipment and the more advanced mission control systems while I flew the ship and handled shielding and weapons. Which, if we were good at our job, we would rarely need.

Ensuring we were both wearing our flight harnesses, I started the engines and requested clearance for takeoff.

Mia rubbed her hands together and stared at the display screen. "Let's go, Kass. I can't wait to see one of the Dark Fleet ships up close."

"They're dangerous, Mia. This isn't a game. The ones we're going after are real."

Was she going to take risks she shouldn't because of the way she'd been trained? I hadn't considered that possibility until this moment. She was a touch reckless. Wild. Just like me. Together, it could be a problem if we weren't careful.

"Oh, I know," she commented. "But that bitch queen tried to kill my best friend and wipe out your entire planet. If what General Jennix said is true, if they wipe out Velerion, Earth will be next on their list of conquests just because Jamie came from there. Me, too. I am not going to let that happen." She shifted in her seat and tilted her head to look at me. Her eyes narrowed, and I was aroused by her vehemence. No one fucked with my pair bond or anyone she cared about. "Not happening. Got it? That bitch is going down."

"So, bonded one, you are not reckless, simply bloodthirsty?" I asked as our ship shot out of the launch area and into open space.

My words made her laugh. "Exactly. Wahooooooo!" she shouted as the G's pushed us into our seats.

She was magnificent. Perfect. Mine. Bloodthirsty, I could work with.

We flew at near top speed on a wide arc toward our target coordinates. Surveillance had tracked a Dark Fleet vessel passing through this area at regular intervals for several days. We would proceed with caution. The regularity of the ship's appearance reeked of a trap. Today, if we were lucky, we'd be close by when they flew through Velerion-controlled space and manage to remain undetected. We would discover what this Dark Fleet ship was doing out here and gather the data General Jennix needed with the Dark Fleet none the wiser.

Mia stared at distant stars, at the darkness of space, and we'd sat in companionable silence for long minutes when she broke the quiet with an unexpected question.

"What's the purpose behind the pair-bonding

thing? In the game I thought it was romantic and fun. But I had no idea other people on Velerion pair bonded as well. Like the mechanics—or mechs, you called them? Vintis and Arria? They're a pair bond, too, right? What does that mean on Velerion? Are we married? Engaged? Do we have some kind of work contract?" Mia's hands flew over her control panel as if she were purposely avoiding eye contact. How she could talk and work proved her insane abilities and complex mind.

I covered her hand with my own and stopped her movement. "Mia, you are mine and I am yours. We worked together, trained together, learned together. We fit one another in skills and temperament. We have common goals and shared work. Pair-bonded Velerion teams are stronger than those who struggle to work alone. Do you not have bonded mates on Earth?"

Mia shrugged. "We do, but it's not like that."

"Then what is your pair bonding like?"

We drifted close to a slowly rotating asteroid, and I placed us in a matching roll so we would look like we were part of the rock.

"Well, humans go out on dates to get to know each other. If they get along and have good chemistry—"

"Chemistry? Between humans? How does this occur? Can you shed your skin? Exchange fluids?"

Mia burst into laughter, but I was serious.

"This is not a joke, Mia. If humans have these types of biological needs for survival, our science and medical teams must be notified. Interpersonal chemical reactions are not in your species reports."

Mia was still smiling as she flipped her hand over so her palm was facing mine. I nearly groaned in contentment as she laced her fingers through mine and bound us into one being. "No. I'm sorry. That is a slang term."

"Slang?"

"Never mind. God, why is this so hard?"

I could give her something hard.

She leaned her head back against the seat. "If the two humans are attracted to one another, they will continue to meet. If they like each other enough, they'll have sex. And if that's good, and they fall in love, they get married, settle down, have a few children, get the house and the dog and the cat and the white picket fence. Go to work, grow old, grow apart, kick the baby out of the house, and fight like injured wolves for the rest of their lives."

I took my time processing what she described. "That sounds horrible."

She laughed again. "It is."

"You meet and talk, then have sex. Then commit to a life bond and begin to procreate? What about sharing common interests and goals? Working together? Becoming stronger as a team? Vintis and Arria are stronger together because they have shared knowledge and work. They help one another solve difficult problems, empathize with one another, understand the challenges each faces. How do your human pair bonds maintain strong relationships if they do not work and learn and strive together?"

"They don't." Mia let go of my hand and sat forward in her seat, inspecting her control panel. "The divorce rate is at least fifty percent."

"What is divorce?"

"The reason I'm not married and never want kids." The bitterness in her voice left me with many unanswered questions, but Mia was correct in her shift of attention. The target vessel had just pinged our ship's sensors and was approaching. I confirmed we were in stealth mode and would never be seen. Still, I had to make one fact clear.

"You are mine, Mia," I said. She would not doubt. Not with me. "You will not pair bond with a human now. We are joined, and I do not share my mate with other males."

Whatever my Mia might be, she was not shy. She turned to look at me, her eyes dark with desire. "I don't share either, flyboy. Just so we're clear."

"I desire no other. The kiss should have made it obvious."

"Good." She turned away from me and pressed the command to slide her seat into MCS mode. "Now let's get going on one of those common goals you were talking about and hack into this asshole's ship systems."

"Agreed. Fight now, fuck later." I waited for the perfect moment to move away from the asteroid and into the passing ship's plasma trail. The *Phantom*'s stealth system was designed to perfectly mimic the frequency of the interstellar plasma flow around it, the quiet hum that would blur our ship into the universe and allow us to evade their sensors.

Mia lifted her gaze to mine, as I'd been expecting, and I slipped *Phantom* to rest within a groove of the Dark Fleet's warship. I'd been expecting something small, a smuggler's shuttle or Scythe fighter on patrol. Instead we were dealing with one of Queen Raya's warships. The ship was massive, larger by half again than the battleship we'd left behind. I'd seen these ships from afar as I lifted troops from battle zones or dropped them off. But I'd never been this close.

Well, not outside of the training simulation.

"It's like a little fish sticking with a whale," she murmured.

I glanced at Mia. Her hands flew over her controls with ease. Her shoulders were relaxed, her gaze focused. I knew the moment she'd accessed their systems by the slight curl at the corner of her lips. When she turned to me, her eyes alight with excitement, I was ready.

"How long do you need?" I whispered. Her response was equally quiet.

"Two minutes. The data transfer is even faster than in the game."

"Of course. Earth's technology is childlike and slow."

"Then why don't you share?" she hissed back.

That was a serious question. "What would your people do with more advanced technology?" I asked.

She shrugged. "That's easy. Kill each other with greater efficiency."

"You have answered your own question."

She turned her head and studied her monitors, hands moving to adjust as the data transfer ebbed and flowed. The silence in the cockpit made me glance over my shoulder. I could not divert my attention from the pilot's controls for long. I had to manually hold us in our current position. Any break and we would be in danger of giving away our location or colliding with their much larger ship.

We worked in silence for long minutes as I used every ounce of skill I possessed to keep us properly aligned with the groove in the giant warship. They were beginning a roll maneuver that I suspected was in preparation for a high-speed exit from the area. We could not be this close to the ship when it decided to go. We'd be destroyed by their engines when they passed by.

"Mia, we have to go."

"I know. I'm almost there." Her entire body buzzed with energy as she leaned forward, fingers and optical controls moving as fast as I'd ever seen her move. Faster than I'd seen in our training simulations.

"Mia." The large ship rolled overhead, and it was now or never.

"Got it! Go!"

I released the magnetic-field-generator pulse I'd been using to assist with our attachment to the warship's outer hull, and the *Phantom* drifted away from the Dark Fleet ship like debris. We rode the ship's plasma distortion wave perfectly.

A strange warning signal sounded. Just once. A ping that made me jolt to attention as Mia's screens filled with interference for several seconds before returning to normal.

The soft alarm stopped.

"What was that?" Mia asked.

"I don't know, but it's gone." I checked every gauge and sensor, everything I could think to inspect as Mia did the same. "Find anything?"

"No. I guess it must have been the plasma field. Or maybe cosmic radiation? Warp core? Solar storm? I'm out of sci-fi words, and I have no idea how this space stuff works. I only know how to run things in this seat. I hated science class."

I was in love. "As did I. If I couldn't fly it or hack into it, I wasn't interested."

"You wanted me bad enough to hack into the *Starfighter Training Academy.*"

"You have no idea," I replied.

"Maybe there really is something to this pair-bond thing."

I grinned. "Give me a couple minutes, and I'll convince you. Again." I glanced at the sensors, relieved to see the warship moving away from us at an increasing pace. No Scythe fighters launched. No communication issues. It appeared we'd accomplished our mission without being detected.

This was so much better than being a shuttle pilot. And with Mia by my side...

A few more minutes and I'd have her all to myself. Getting her naked would be my top priority.

7

A FEW MORE MINUTES? I craved him now. I squirmed in my chair at his promises. With that ping not repeating itself, I let the adrenaline course through me. We were away from the Dark Fleet ship, and we had the data.

We'd completed a real mission.

"Is it always like that?" I asked.

"Like what?" Kass replied, monitoring the ship's course back to the *Resolution*.

"Like... insane. Exhilarating. Soooo much better than the game."

Of course, we had sneaked in and sneaked out

undetected. We hadn't used any of the fighting skills we'd practiced in the game. But still... it was *real.*

I looked out the window at space. *Space.* Would I ever get used to this? There was no green. No blue sky. I wondered what it was like on Velerion. Was it like Earth? The *Starfighter Training Academy* didn't reference the home planet much. Since we were stationed on a battleship, it wasn't as if I was going to find out anytime soon. And based on the data we'd just uncovered, we were likely going to be at the center of the latest battle with the Dark Fleet.

Now that we were done, I was antsy. I felt like I couldn't sit still, which was pretty difficult in a space-ship. There was nowhere to go.

"What's the matter, my Mia?"

"I'm... happy," I admitted, and a slow smile crept across my face. "No, it's more than that. Thrilled. It's nothing like playing in my living room. You were there with me then, but I didn't know you were real."

"Do you need a reminder?"

Definitely not. I knew he was real. So did my body. But I was across the galaxy staring out at space. It was like I was another person, completely different than who I'd been just a few days ago. But that version of me was real, too. Kass had been on Earth. He'd seen my other life. And saved me from it.

Literally swept me off my feet, up against the door, and then to another planet.

"Mia? I want you. Naked. Now."

I flushed all over, and my core clenched. He wasn't tame, that was for sure. And I liked him that way. I glanced at my sensors one last time to make sure we were totally and completely alone out here.

"Kassius Remeas?"

"Naked, Mia."

"I know you're real."

"Indeed."

"So is your magical cock," I countered, sorting the data I'd downloaded into manageable packets.

"Magical?" He laughed.

"I can't believe we just did that. So surreal."

"Very real. Now the general's people can analyze the data and plan an attack."

"How are they going to blow up the IPBMs without destroying an entire planet?"

"That's for Jennix and the others to figure out. In the past, our science teams suggested we fire them into our star, Vega. That is not for us to worry about. When we get back, we are required to rest."

I glanced at him, and I heard the deeper timbre of his voice.

"Rest?"

"Sleep. As a pilot I am required to recharge for a duration of twelve hours prior to a new mission. You as well."

"Do we have to... rest the entire time?"

He gave the controls one more glance, then shifted to give me all his attention. "Do you have battle lust?"

I frowned. "What?"

His dark gaze roved over me. Every inch, and his attention made my nipples tingle. "It is when a fight is over that my cock is hard. I need to fuck. Quick. Hard. Dirty. It bleeds off the adrenaline."

"I don't have a cock," I countered.

He winked. "I'm well aware of what you *have.*"

I bit my lip. "I don't know if it's battle desire or what, but I do need you. Now. I can't wait until we get back to our quarters."

He unclipped his harness. "Then we won't."

"What?" When he crooked his finger, I looked around. "Here?" He'd told me to get naked, but I'd thought he was just teasing. Flirting. Increasing the anticipation.

My body liked the idea, but the *Phantom* was small. *Really* small.

"Here. Now. You're going to climb onto my lap

and you're going to ride my cock until you come at least twice."

I narrowed my eyes, equally turned on and appalled. No one had ever talked to me like that before, not without being throat punched. "Is that a command, Starfighter?"

He cocked his head. "Do you want me to boss you around?"

Did I? We'd had sex within ten minutes of meeting each other. Only a door had separated us from my coworkers. Now there was no one around. There was *nothing* around.

I needed the connection with Kass. His touch. The feel of him inside me. Of knowing we were alive. And I needed it now.

"Oh yeah," I said.

"That's 'yes, sir, Starfighter,'" he countered. When his voice went that deep and dominating, I shivered.

I also unbuckled my seat harness and climbed onto my knees. It was like getting undressed in a big SUV. There was *some* room but not much. I bumped a display screen with my elbow, kneed something else, got my foot caught for a second, but got naked. Flight-suit battle armor wasn't easy to strip out of.

Lesson learned. But the way Kass watched me

was worth it because when I was finally bare, he licked his lips and the heat in his gaze was scorching.

He opened his pants, lifted his hips, and pushed the material down. Damn him, that was all he had to do for his cock to spring free.

I crawled over everything to get to him. His hands came around my waist to help me.

Then I was there. In his lap. Straddling him so that my back was to his controls and the front window. All I could see was Kass.

Then I couldn't see him at all because his mouth was on mine in a searing kiss. Hot, carnal. Wild.

He broke his mouth away, and with a hand pressed to the center of my chest, he tipped me back into his controls as he sucked a nipple. Hard. I arched my back and gasped, tangled my fingers in his dark hair.

"This is on autopilot, right?" I asked, my eyes closed, the pleasure from my nipple zinging right to my core. God, I was going to come like this. "We're not going to fly into an asteroid or anything?"

He came off my nipple with a loud pop, and I blinked my eyes open. He leaned to the left, checked the controls. "No. And if you're thinking about that, I'm not doing this right."

"How this works is you put your cock in my pussy."

A grin spread across his face as his hand came down on my ass in a hard swat.

Heat flared along with the sting. Holy shit, he'd spanked me!

"Who's in control here?"

"You."

"You want my cock?"

I looked down between us where it was long and thick and dripping pre-cum. I wanted to lick that drop off, but I was an MCS, not a contortionist.

"Yes."

"Then lift up your hips and take it."

I did as he said, pushing up on my knees and gripping him at the base. Lowering down, I didn't wait, only notched him at my entrance, then settled him deep.

Once he was fully inside, he bucked up and I went with him. My hand slapped back on the controls for balance.

I smiled, then let my eyes roll back. "Yes. Harder."

He gripped my hips, lifted me, and dropped me down as he angled his hips up. We slapped together, flesh against flesh as I cried out. Only the sounds of our fucking filled the starfighter's small cabin... *Yes. Harder. You like it rough, don't you? Your cock's so big. I need every inch. Take it. I'm coming!*

It wasn't long for either of us to come. He was right. Sex after a mission was intense and frenzied and so, so good. My mind was already making excuses for my out-of-control reaction to him. Otherwise I'd have to say this voracious need for Kass was too much. Who fucked like rabbits in a spaceship?

Me.

I was a total space hussy. And that made me smile.

Sweaty and satisfied, I slumped in Kass's arms. "Next time we'll—"

"Do it in your private quarters."

I froze at the strange voice coming through the comms.

Shit. Someone had heard us. I looked to Kass, who appeared a little contrite, but he was still smiling.

"Starfighters, this is the *Battleship Resolution,* MCS command. Now that you're finished, disengage autopilot and return to base."

Kass leaned forward, his cheek brushing my breast, to press a button. One it seemed I'd sat on and activated with my ass.

"Affirmative," Kass said, his finger hovering over the button. "Returning to base."

He pushed the button, and I dropped my forehead to his chest. He was still inside me, and I was completely naked.

"We're screwed," I said.

"You definitely were. And you will be again once we get back to our quarters."

"We're in such big trouble."

"Maybe. Doubtful," he said. He glanced at my discarded flight suit. "How long will it take you to get back into your clothes?"

I did the mental math. "Maybe five minutes, if you count the boots."

With a grin, he leaned forward, both arms around me, and I had to cling to him, shoving my breast into the side of his face to prevent myself from falling backward again. "What are you doing?"

"Putting the ship on autopilot."

"Why? They said to turn off autopilot and return to base."

He nipped at the outer edge of my breast, and my body reacted with a jolt of need that had my wet heat in spasms around his hard length. "Because the ride home is over an hour through heavily protected Velerion space, so I have us in stealth mode, so no one can see us anyway, and—" He finished whatever he was doing behind me and leaned back into his seat, one hand lifted to cup my jaw, the other at the curve of my lower back.

"And?"

He leaned in and kissed me, this time gentle, unhurried. I felt like I was being worshipped. Craved. Loved. "And I'm not finished with you yet."

Using my inner muscles, I squeezed his cock over and over again until he groaned, his kissing becoming wild. Desperate. Uncontrolled. I tried to tell him what I was feeling with my hands and mouth, but something had happened to me. I was broken, every shield I'd built around my heart tumbling to ruin like rocks in a landslide. I was shaking. Tears ran from the corners of my eyes, and I had no idea where they came from. It was like my body was crying for me.

Kass shifted his hips, and I moaned in encouragement but didn't let go of the kiss. Where we'd both been out of control the first time, this was slow. Deliberate. Full of emotion and longing and contentment.

This was *not* me. I did not believe in fairy tales, true love, finding *the One*, and soul mates. I'd watched my parents grow to hate one another, keeping me trapped in their house because they were staying together—for me. My colleagues, one after another, came home after a trip abroad or a long mission to find a coldly worded note or an empty closet and divorce papers. Love was a lie created by chemicals in the brain designed to drive human beings to procreate.

But fuck me, the lie felt so good. I *wanted* to believe this was real, that Kass adored me, needed me, loved me.

He wrapped his hand around the back of my neck and held me in place. I blinked up into those dark eyes, completely in his thrall. He could ask me for anything right now, and I'd want to give it to him.

"I can feel you thinking, my Mia."

I denied nothing but didn't lay my soul bare at his feet, either. Silence was often the best answer. With a lingering kiss, he moved his other hand between us, his thumb moving closer and closer to my clit.

"No more thinking." He placed a soft kiss on each eyelid before pulling me forward so his lips hovered above my ear. "I'm going to make you come now, love. Again and again until you beg me to stop."

I scoffed. I couldn't help the reaction. "That'll be never."

He tugged on my earlobe with his lips. "I do love a challenge."

I squirmed at the tone of his voice and blushed because I'd never been so wild for someone before. I'd never been this insatiable. Sex was sex. An orgasm made me relax, but with Kass, it was so much more. And I couldn't get enough.

When we landed and walked down the ramp just over an hour later, my knees were shaky and I still had not regained control of my breathing. I had to be a mess. Flushed. Swollen lips. Glazed eyes. But I realized, with no small bit of satisfaction, that Kass hadn't even bothered to run his fingers through his hair. As well fucked as I looked, he looked like he'd literally just rolled out of bed.

Unrepentant. No apologies or excuses or shame.

Vintis and Arria walked to us with huge smiles on their faces. "How'd the ship do?"

"There was a glitch for a few seconds. Whole system. Screens went blank, then everything seemed to be normal," I said.

Arria frowned. "I'll get on that. Track every line and connection personally."

"Thank you."

Vintis was watching Kass. "You have any trouble, sir?"

Kass looked down at me, then back to the ship with a considering look on his face. "No. But I do have some interior modifications I'd like to discuss with you."

Arria giggled and I realized Kass intended to make sure the next time we had sex on the ship, it was more comfortable.

With a grin that was pure happiness, Arria pointed to the outer landing bay where the rest of the *Resolution's* ships were kept. "You better get going. The general has been pacing for almost an hour."

Great.

Kass squeezed my hand, and we walked shoulder to shoulder into the main landing bay. Everyone there, from mechanics to cleaning crews, turned our way and clapped. A few whistled, and everyone was grinning.

And it wasn't because we'd hacked into the Dark Fleet system and collected the data.

No, it was because I'd sat on a comms button with my bare ass and broadcast a live porno. I slowed my steps, realizing it was possible it had been heard by all of Velerion and its bases around the universe.

That would be bad. How many bases or whatever did Velerion have, exactly?

"How far do our ship comms go?" I asked Kass.

"They are on a closed frequency to the *Resolution*."

I sighed with relief as Kass tugged me close. "No one will doubt our bond now, my Mia. Relax. We're good."

I rolled my eyes. "Based on the response, I'd say we were better than good."

He laughed and wrapped his arm around me, then kissed the top of my head. He led me through the throng, accepting some ribbing and innuendo good-naturedly. I smiled and while I was embarrassed, I was also proud.

Everyone knew we were pair bonded now. *Everyone* knew it was a good match. Kass was happy, and I wasn't ashamed of us.

Damn proud.

ia, Two Days Later, Battleship Resolution

"Settle in and settle down, everyone," General Jennix called.

The Starfighters and other crew members serving on the *Resolution* who would be involved in the mission moved into chairs lined up in rows around the meeting room. I guessed there were about twenty present and at least double that amount of people attending remotely via the comms covering the walls around the room.

"To make introductions. From Arturri, we have General Aryk and the Starfighter pilots. They will be

known as Group One. From Eos Station, Captain
Sponder is leading the shuttle pilots." The general
paused. "Where is Captain Sponder?"

I didn't see the jerk on the screen either. It had
been two days since I'd met Kass's former
commanding officer. Sponder had been an asshole,
and it was clear he hated Kass.

That fact did not bother me. Sponder was one of
those guys who always felt the need to throw their
dicks on the table and get out the measuring tape.
I'd met plenty of jerks just like him back on Earth.
Hot hunks. Creeps. Dedicated soldiers. Uptight
commanders. Rebels. It seemed people were people,
no matter what planet they were on.

Kass, for his part, hadn't mentioned Sponder
since that initial encounter. After our mission, we'd
gone back to our quarters and rested, as protocol
required. But Kass had made good on his promise of
taking me again once we were in bed. He'd bathed
me, had food brought to our quarters, then sexed me
into unconsciousness. I wasn't sure if that was how
Jennix wanted us to rest, but it was a great way to fall
asleep. I was now fresh, relaxed, and ready for
another mission.

"We don't know, sir." One of the shuttle pilots
under Captain Sponder's command answered the

general, and I pulled my wandering thoughts back under control. This was a huge mission. Important. If something went wrong, it wasn't going to be because I missed something or made a mistake. Not again. Never again.

Jennix sighed. "Very well. The shuttle pilots are Group Two. They will be running supplies and evacuation operations from the launch bays on the *Resolution*. General Romulus and the Starfighter Titans are Group Three. They will focus their attack on the IPBM production facility once the MCS team takes down the shield and their moon-based defense systems. Captain Dacron and her medical teams are Group Four. They will set up a triage area in the *Resolution's* cargo bay until we gain ground control on the planet. Once that is done, they will set up in Alpha City, under the largest dome. I am General Jennix, in command of our new Starfighter MCS team. Several squadrons of fighters from other battleships as well as air support for the assault will be under my command. We are Group Five."

Each group appeared to be in rooms similar to ours and stationed somewhere around Velerion. I didn't recognize any faces except for Jamie's and Alex's, who were seated behind their general, Aryk, on one of the screens. I wanted to wave and say hi, but I knew that was bad. Sex on the *Phantom* at the end of a mission was one thing. Interrupting General Jennix to give a shout-out to a BFF during a briefing was another.

"As usual, to simplify, all leaders will be identified solely by their group, meaning for this mission I am Group Five Leader."

Heads nodded. I was thankful because I was terrible with names. If I had to remember them to communicate, I'd be in big trouble.

"Here is what we know," Jennix continued. She motioned to Graves, and a large, three-dimensional hologram appeared in the middle of the room. The image was of a barren planet that looked like nothing but black rocks with a few, small domes built on the surface. The planet had bluish ice caps on each pole and one large moon. I glanced up at the screens to see that identical formations had appeared in front of each group.

I leaned toward Kass and whispered in his ear.

"What is that on the planet? Ice?"

"Yes. The Vega System contains large amounts of water."

"Why is it blue instead of white?"

"Methane."

And I was done with asking questions. Chemistry was not my area. Still, the planet was oddly beautiful with its dark rock and bright blue caps.

"Why is Jennix leading the mission?"

"Because the MCS group has the data, sets the parameters and requirements for the mission. Identifies the resources needed. The battleship will also act as the forward operations center, close enough to offer support but just out of range in case those missiles detonate. So, Jennix is in charge," he whispered back.

That made sense.

General Jennix cleared her throat and looked straight at me.

"Sorry, General."

She continued. "The data collected by the Starfighter MCS pair indicates the location of the IPBM production facility is Velerion's colony, Xenon. As most of you know, Xenon was overrun by Dark Fleet forces eight months ago. With the catastrophic losses to our Starfighter teams, we have not been in a position to launch an assault and regain control."

I assumed the history lesson was for me and Jamie, the only two outsiders in the room. However, we also happened to be Starfighters critical to this mission.

Whispers came from all groups, and Jennix

allowed everyone a moment to process the information. While I hadn't been in space long, the IPBM
issue had been a problem since Jamie had been
captured. No one had been able to discover the
precise location of Queen Raya's stockpile or
production facility. Until now.

"Our colonists have also been under Dark Fleet
control for the last eight months. Xenon's moon base
was converted into a planetwide defense system.
Once we knew where to look, we sent multiple
drones to the planet in order to scout out what we
might be up against."

Jennix waved her hand in the air and the holographic planet became larger, but the single moon
grew exponentially until we were looking at a long,
arc-shaped base of some kind that rested on its
surface. It looked like a giant black centipede with a
tall, arching back.

"The moon base houses two unique weapons.
The first is an energy shield generator. The force
field created by this technology makes movement to
and from the Xenon's surface impossible. The
second is a planetwide, low-frequency broadcast
technology we believe they are using to keep the
colonists on Xenon complacent or weakened in

some way. A form of subtle manipulation or mind control."

That caused a stir, and even Kass stiffened next to me.

"The moon base is, according to reports, unmanned and run by an automated defense system that is monitored remotely. We believe our Starfighter MCS team can get in close enough to the moon base in their ship to take down both systems. The energy shield and the mind-control frequencies are broadcast simultaneously. If we can eliminate one, we should eliminate both."

What the hell? Mind-control frequency? Broadcast over an entire planet from one small base on one moon?

I nudged Kass again. "Does Earth have any of this stuff? This technology?"

He rubbed the top of my thigh with his palm. "I don't know. It's possible. Velerion would not have shared this technology. It's been outlawed for centuries by the Galactic Alliance. But Queen Raya doesn't exactly follow the rules. And our intelligence teams reported that she is interested in Earth for a future conquest."

What a bitch. Would she set up a mind-control

beam from Earth's moon? To do what? "What does that technology do?"

General Jennix heard me and answered my question. "It generates fear frequencies and blankets the planet. They can't be heard, but the energy affects the subconscious mind. It makes people sad, tired, depressed, angry, and hopeless. Mostly hopeless."

"So they won't fight back."

"So they won't fight back," she confirmed.

Scheisse.

She continued addressing everyone. "As you know, Xenon's surface is not habitable. Only the five domed cities in the southern region can sustain life, and they cover a small area. The population of the planet is minimal. Less than fifty thousand. It was thought that Queen Raya would use the planet as an operational base, but she has not done so. We now believe Xenon was taken solely to be used as a production facility for IPBMs."

"They wanted Xenon's ore and factories," Group Four Leader offered.

"Correct." Jennix nodded. "And the highly trained workforce."

"Slaves," someone said.

"Prisoners of war," Jennix corrected. "Soon to be liberated."

Fifty thousand people were on that planet? That many prisoners forced to work for Queen Raya? And every single one of those lives depended on me to liberate them?

The air in the room grew too hot. Stifling.

Kass squeezed my leg, and I settled enough to listen in again.

"Since Xenon was enslaved, Queen Raya has had thousands of laborers at her disposal to quickly convert the factory and produce the IPBMs. They have focused their attention on missile production."

"How does the Dark Fleet control the people if they don't have a base?" Group Four Leader asked.

"The moon base station is their primary means of maintaining control. Data grids were installed to put a force field around the planet. Nothing can get through. No comms. No shuttles. They are under a net of Dark Fleet power. However, based on the drone data we were able to analyze, we believe they have at least two squadrons of Scythe fighters as well as significant ground forces on the surface. Taking the force field down will be the beginning of the battle, not the end of it."

"How will this work?" one of the shuttle pilots asked.

"The MCS pair will hover over the moon base

and shut down the force field and frequency generators. This will allow the Starfighter pilots, the Titans, and our remaining ground forces to access Xenon's airspace. The shuttle pilots will follow with the ground forces. Once they land on the planet and are deployed, we will coordinate air and land strikes."

"If we blow up the IPBMs at the factory, we'll blow up the planet," Group One Leader commented.

"We intend to launch the IPBMs and fire them into our star, Vega," Kass said, his voice carrying. "Vega can absorb the energy of those missiles and remain unaffected."

Jennix looked to Kass. "That is correct. The remainder of the mission debrief will be led by Kass and Mia, our new, and only, Starfighter MCS pair."

Kass stood and I blinked at him. We were leading an entire mission? Yes. I knew we would. We had in the game. But in real life there were lives at risk. This wasn't sexy times. This was life or death.

I popped to my feet, not wanting to embarrass Kass or the general.

Kass took my hand and led me to the front of the room to stand beside Jennix.

"Group Two will lead shuttle missions to drop Titans in various locations around the biosphere cities on Xenon to guard the citizens and our shuttle teams against a ground assault. As soon as the force field goes down, the Scythe fighter squadrons will be scrambled. We need our Starfighter pilots to be ready to lead them away from the missile facility.

"Shuttle pilots will bring in a crew of scientists and weapons specialists who will enter the production plant and fire the live IPBMs toward Vega."

"Isn't it easier to aim them at an asteroid belt?" a shuttle pilot asked.

"Good question. It would be, but debris from the missile strikes would spread across the system. We would be dodging it for years, and we do not need a random asteroid or large meteor shower to hit Velerion."

The pilot grinned somewhat sheepishly. "That would be bad."

Kass nodded. "Affirmative. Mia and I will take down the shield on the moon base station, which will free Xenon from Dark Fleet control. Group leaders have been sent instructions and further details in order to ready your crews. Once the force field goes down, all other crews will be a go to engage."

Jennix nodded. "Group Two shuttles, you will drop your teams and remain in Xenon airspace, on standby, for retrieval or assistance if necessary. The rest of the details are in your mission briefs."

Kass looked between the comms and the group present. "We can now break into smaller groups to identify specific team tasks."

Kass looked to me.

I made eye contact with every team member in the room and on every screen. I was superstitious that way, but I liked to know who I was going into the field—or into space—with. "Stay sharp and stay safe."

General Jennix placed her hands on her hips. "Group leaders, anything to add?"

"I have something to add."

This time it really was Sponder who spoke, but he wasn't on the comm with his team, instead he was here. In person. Everyone swiveled to look at him.

"Captain, why are you not at Eos Station?" Jennix asked. "We have a mission to run."

"Because *my* mission is to see him in the brig." He pointed at Kass.

Kass sighed.

Arsch. Sponder was always in the way, and I'd barely met the guy.

"And I told you he is no longer under your

command," Jennix added. "He is now a Starfighter MCS."

"He accessed Velerion data cores without consent. He did not have clearance. We do not know the extent of his breach."

"Again, it shows his skill as an MCS. An asset to the fight against the Dark Fleet."

"I disagree," Sponder countered. "He is a menace. A threat to all of Velerion, especially since he hacked in to change the scores on his data in the Starfighter Training Academy."

What? I turned away from Sponder to study Kass. He scowled like he was ready to commit cold-blooded murder. I couldn't blame him. But I also wanted to know if Sponder's accusation was true.

"Are you saying he cheated?" Jennix asked.

Kass had admitted to hacking into the training program to be added to the possible matches, but not cheating to complete the training levels and graduate. To pair bond with me. To fight with me. Was it all a lie then? Had I been duped by someone I trusted? *Again?* Was my bad judgment about to get more people killed on this mission?

Maybe I should have stayed behind the desk back in Berlin where no one was hurt if I trusted the wrong person.

Kass's back went stiff. "I did no such thing."

"And we are to believe you?" Sponder asked, his brow raised.

Jennix's shoulders dropped. "I think your accusations are far-fetched, Captain."

"I do not." The man with Sponder, who I'd pretty much ignored until now, spoke. "I am Commissioner Gaius."

I'd never heard of the title *commissioner* before. It hadn't been in the game. Based on his age and the formal style of his clothes—he looked like an anime character with spiked hair, fancy boots and a long, stylized jacket decorated with elaborately designed buttons—he was some kind of bureaucrat or politician. And since he was bickering with Jennix, he was most likely her superior. That meant Sponder was so determined to take down Kass that he'd pulled rank and gone over the general's head.

I glanced at Kass. He was following the action just like everyone else in the room, and on the comms, but his gaze was on Sponder and Kass wasn't even trying to hide his hatred.

This was different. Kass's jaw was clenched, and he looked not just livid but shocked. Outraged.

"The captain has shared his concerns with me,

and I have inspected the data core records reviewed this MCS's access."

"How did the captain access the data core records? A captain doesn't have that level of clearance," Jennix countered.

"I do," Commissioner Gaius said, eyes narrowing. Clearly he didn't like to be doubted. "I looked into the matter personally." He turned to Kass. "Starfighter MCS Kassius Remeas not only accessed the training program to include himself, but he falsified the training mission data. The accuracy and validity of their training scores has come into question. I, personally, do not believe Kassius Remeas completed the training program, and have asked the military commissioners to initiate a full review of his service record."

Kass held up a hand, looked from Gaius to Jennix. "I openly admitted to hacking in, but I deny the rest. We completed the training."

Gaius didn't seem to care what Kass had to say. "Kassius Remeas, you are under arrest for violating the breach of secrets, accessing data core information beyond your rank, violating a commanding officer's direct order, and more."

Jennix stepped forward, blocking the guards who

entered the room at the flick of Gaius's wrist. Over the commissioner's shoulder, I saw Sponder's smirk.

"Not until the mission is complete," Jennix said. "Commissioner, you have to be aware of the IPBM threat to Velerion. MCS Remeas and Becker discovered the location of the factory and how the Dark Fleet is controlling it. Keeping him from the mission will hurt us."

"He has been of service," Gaius said. "But to allow him to breach protocol in such an egregious way, and then lead all these teams? No. I will not take that risk. Can you personally guarantee they have the skill necessary to lead such a crucial mission? Cheating means they did not do the work. They did not complete the training. Therefore the lives of all team members would be in jeopardy." He flicked his wrist toward the comms behind her. Jennix didn't turn.

"Arrest him after the mission. Have guards in the docking bay waiting for his return."

She had more faith in Kass than anyone else.

More than I did, apparently.

While Kass denied Sponder's claims, he *had* hacked into the training system. It would make sense for him to also be able to manipulate the game itself. Had he felt the need to cheat because I wasn't actually good enough? Had I completed the levels of the game not because I'd been gaining skill, but because Kass had been hacking the game to guarantee our success?

I looked at Kass. He was still glaring at Sponder.

Gaius stepped toward me, looked me over from head to toe. As if he were searching for—and expecting to find—weakness. "MCS Becker, unfortunately your status as a Starfighter is now in question. Do you deserve to be here? Are you any good?"

I lifted my chin and met his gaze. Refused to look away. I'd felt like this before, when my abilities were doubted. When I'd trusted an informant, believed his lies, and led a team into an ambush. We'd lost two lives that day. I'd blamed myself, and I wasn't alone. Everyone else had blamed me as well. I'd been demoted, put on a desk job. Nearly fired.

My skill with a computer had saved my career, if not assuaged my guilt. But this time I had no answer. I had no idea if Kass and I had actually completed the missions and won on our own merits, or if he'd cheated and dragged me along for the ride.

Was I good enough? Or was this another lie I'd swallowed, told by another liar I'd trusted with my life as well as the lives of others?

I hated myself a bit for doubting Kass, but I'd been in this situation before.

Gaius looking down his nose at me was the icing on the cake, and I had nothing to say to him. Not. One. Word.

"Take him away. He is a disgrace to the Starfighter uniform," Gaius said with another flick of his wrist.

A pair of guards surrounded Kass.

I didn't know what to do. What to believe.

Had he really done it? Cheated to be an MCS? It had nothing to do with me, his ambition. I didn't blame him for wanting to be away from Sponder, but had he really taken it to this extreme?

I was hurt. Not physically, but was I here because Kass had cheated instead of for my abilities? Was this Berlin all over again? Was I just collateral damage of an alien male's power trip?

Kass was swiftly cuffed, but he didn't make it easy. Sponder stepped close to Kass. While the captain was shorter, he must have felt as if he had the upper hand. Especially since Kass's hands were restrained behind his back.

"Not much of an MCS now," Sponder said. "You'll go down as a Velerion without honor."

Kass glared, then whipped his head forward,

headbutting the fucker right in the nose. Holy shit. Blood spurted everywhere, and I stepped back. Sponder howled in pain and clutched his—most likely broken—nose.

The guards yanked on Kass and started to push him out of the room.

Scheisse.

Gaius and Sponder followed, leaving a vacuum of silence. Then everyone started talking at once.

"Quiet!" Jennix raised her arms, and silence quickly returned.

Jennix swore under her breath, stared at the ground for a bit. No one moved. No one practically blinked while we waited. I was silent because I was stunned. I wasn't in Germany where I could go back to my apartment, put on some sweats, and eat ice cream until I felt better after dealing with a colleague. I was in space. I hadn't even been here a week and... *scheisse.* The only guy I'd wanted, depended on, craved, trusted—hell, even loved— was something I hadn't expected.

Hacking and pushing boundaries was one thing. That I could respect. But manipulating training programs when other people's lives were at stake? When the consequences affected more than just him? Hell, the consequences of his cheating *gave* me to him. For life.

Pair bonded. Permanently together.

But what happened when the bond was created by a lie? When we hadn't earned the right? When we hadn't actually completed the missions? The training? Was I still a Starfighter if Kass was not?

What happened now? Did I go back to Earth? I held my breath, waiting for Jennix to say something.

"While that was... unpleasant," she said, cutting into my thoughts, "the mission will proceed, as planned, in eight hours. All of you are required to rest, then coordinate with your team leaders. Support crews will be making preparations while you do."

"Wait. Don't you wonder if I'm good enough?" I asked her but spoke to everyone.

"We don't have time to test you. You're the best we've got."

"You're not sending me back to Earth?"

Jennix's eyes widened. "No. Why would you assume that?"

"I might not actually belong here."

I was no longer proud of what I'd accomplished. We might have been the only MCS pair bond, but we were shamed. My abilities were in question.

Everyone on the mission would wonder if I might let them down. Let them die.

"MCS Remeas will be investigated. The truth will become apparent. The mission must go on. The IPBM threat must be eliminated."

"But how—" I began. Jennix cut me off. I'd never flown with anyone but Kass. I'd only had him by my side for every level of the game. I knew nothing else. Could I even do my job with a stranger, no matter his or her skill? Could I do my job at all? They were counting on me to take down the moon base's force field and frequency generators.

"You will have a new flight partner, a pilot," she said. "Obviously it won't be Kass, but a qualified pilot nonetheless, the best we can find. He or she will be assigned prior to the mission."

I stepped closer, spoke softly so others couldn't hear. "What about our pair bond? I mean, is it even real? If he cheated, would he even be allowed to stay bonded with me? What's going to happen between the two of us?"

She offered me a soft smile. Not of a general but of a female.

Jennix pitied me. Just like if I'd been cheated on back on Earth. Kass hadn't had an affair or anything like that, but the entire basis for our relationship was built on a lie. I'd told him about Earth dating and marriages and how I didn't trust them. How could I trust our pair bond? Was there a pair-bond divorce?

"Rest, MCS Becker. You have a job to do soon," she said.

I could only nod. I wasn't familiar with the dynamics of the Velerion military. I'd never been a soldier, not like the rest of the group members. But I knew to be respectful. I thought I knew my place out here in space. It was in the MCS chair on the *Phantom.*

Right?

9

*M*ia, Battleship Resolution, *Personal Quarters*

I WAS EXPECTED TO SLEEP. It was actually required. I agreed, in theory. But the mission had been laid out and they expected us to just shut off all the plans, all the anxiety that went with something so dangerous, and *sleep?* And that was just the mission. That didn't even take into account the rest.

General Jennix expected me to go to the moon base and disarm the Dark Fleet controls by hacking in from the *Phantom* after my pair bond was arrested and thrown in the brig? For being a cheater?

I laid in bed staring up at the ceiling. Willing

myself to wind down and sleep. It wasn't happening. The sheets were a tangle around my legs, and I turned onto my side. Stared at the wall. What was I going to do without Kass in the pilot seat? Could I even hack and take down the force field over Xenon? Was I even qualified? What if I failed? What if I actually couldn't do it and Kass had done things to the training program to make me succeed?

I now questioned everything I'd done in the game. Because everything I'd done had been with Kass.

Had he been using me?

Scheisse.

Everyone was counting on me. On us, whoever the other half of the new MCS pair was.

Us was supposed to be me and Kass. But now I had no idea what was real and what wasn't.

I paused, thought about what *was* real.

Kass had admitted he'd hacked his way into the Starfighter program. That was fact. Sponder hated him. From what Kass had said, for a long time. When I'd first arrived on the battleship, Sponder was there. Waiting. He'd discovered Kass's shift to the MCS group while Kass had been on Earth. Sponder hadn't mentioned cheating then. He must've had someone look into it after that. But why? Jennix had been the one to tell Sponder off, not Kass. I'd even sassed him. Sponder didn't like to be humiliated. That was fact, too.

Why was Sponder such a dick? Had he always been one, or just to Kass?

Kass was cocky. He bent the rules. Literally flew by the seat of his pants. Hacking into the *Starfighter Training Academy* and adding himself as a potential match wasn't the end of the world. Jennix didn't even seem to care.

But cheating? Humans and Velerions had similar notions of honor.

Kass was rebellious, without doubt. But a cheat? A liar? Something just wasn't right.

If Jennix wanted me to sleep, too bad. I climbed from the bed, threw on some clothes. A glance at the clock told me well over an hour had passed as my brain churned. Yeah, I'd rested.

Now it was time to get to work. If Kass had broken into the system, there would be a path to follow, data and records showing him adding himself to the training program. Invisible bread crumbs of sorts. I'd find them. I'd also find out exactly how he had cheated.

If Sponder had found it, I definitely could. And why had Sponder wasted time looking? The IPBMs were a huge problem. Everyone was working around the clock to deal with the issue. So why was Sponder so focused instead on Kass? A cheater was bad news, sure. But shouldn't Sponder be focused on the most crucial issue of saving his planet?

And why would he pull in that old guy? The commissioner. Sponder knew about the mission. He was the leader of Group Two. Yet he'd left his base and those under his command to deal with Kass instead. Here on the *Resolution*.

There were answers here, and I was going to find them. Kass had showed me that the main computer controls were in the wall. But there was a portable unit, like a laptop, that could be pulled from it to work more efficiently. I took it from the small docking station beneath the comm display and went to the couch. Setting it on the low table before me, I got to work.

This was my element. A comms screen, a keyboard, and access to data. Lots of data. I began to work my way through it, starting with the basic bio on Kass. When his smiling face came up on the screen, I ached for him. My body, sure, but my heart, too. When I'd accepted him as a pair bond, I hadn't known he was real. I'd thought him part of a game.

I'd loved him. Even then. But now? Now I

followed the trail. Dug back to the day I'd started the game, when I'd chosen Kass by answering a partner questionnaire. I found his access even before then. His acceptance into the program. He'd been waiting.

It showed it wasn't me specifically he'd targeted. He was one of a long list of matches. It was my random data that matched to his. Statistically it was almost impossible for us to have been put together. But we had.

Then I searched our training data. The scores at each level.

I stilled. Froze.

There it was. The original scores. The modified ones. The edits to the game code that made each level easier. Shorter. Gave additional lives. Points. All the advantages we'd need to win.

Scheisse. He'd cheated. It was all right there.

I leaned back on the couch. It was true. Sponder wasn't lying.

God, I hated Kass. I loved him, but I hated him for it. He'd made me believe. Made me think I was different. Special. Important.

But I was just as Sponder had said. Less than. Not worthy.

Somehow I had to push past my self-doubt. No one could deny I was good at hacking. On Earth and here as part of Velerion's team. I didn't trust people, but I trusted data. Could find it. Understand the ebbs and flows, find patterns.

And something about this data was... off. Wrong. The feeling was pure instinct, and I didn't try to deny it. Something about this entire situation was strange. Too personal. And data was not personal. Data was the absolute. Impartial. It didn't lie.

I couldn't trust Kass, and I'd thought him worthy of it. I'd never trusted Sponder.

I had no one else. No one had my back here. Sure, Jamie did, but she was based on Arturri. It wasn't the same. I was on my own. So I let my fingers fly. I read. I cross-referenced. I correlated all the information, saved documents. News reports. I focused first on Sponder, then Commissioner Gaius. Discovered the programmer who had created the *Starfighter Training Academy*.

That was one genius I'd like to meet.

Sponder. That bastard had his fingerprints all over the place. And not just on Eos Station. His record went back more than a decade, and it was all a little too neat and tidy. Except for his issues with Kass, it seemed he had a squeaky clean, perfect record.

An asshole like that? Yeah, right. He had friends

in high places, that's what Captain Sponder, *nephew of Commissioner Gaius,* had going for him. Nepotism at its finest and the chip on his shoulder to go with it.

"Starfighter Becker."

I blinked, so entrenched in the data I thought I heard my name.

"Starfighter Becker."

I had. "Yes," I called, realizing I was being paged through the comms system.

"Report to duty on the flight deck."

Report for duty? Now? I looked to the time, discovered hours had passed. I'd learned a lot about Sponder. Things he didn't want anyone to know. He was a dick, but even though that was fact, everyone knew it. There was more. I was close to something big on him. I was exhilarated, amped on adrenaline. It was there, hovering in the data. Something was off about him.

"I just need more time," I murmured.

"Negative," the voice replied even though I hadn't been speaking to her. "The mission begins in thirty minutes. You must be in your starfighter in fifteen. General Jennix wants you to meet your new pilot."

I glanced at the comm unit, even though it was

only a voice transmission, not video. My new partner. I swallowed hard. I'd forgotten, lost in data. "Yes. I'll be there."

I stood, stared down at the pseudo-laptop. It was in my nature to keep going. To keep digging until I had the answers. But the mission was more important. Kass had cheated. The data was there that proved it. He wouldn't be flying with me. I also didn't have the evidence—yet—that Sponder was more of a tool than Kass had said.

I'd get the data. I'd get Sponder. And then I'd get Kass. Because I was pissed. He'd messed with the wrong woman. I just had to help save a planet first.

———

KASS, *Cell T-492*

GAIUS AND SPONDER accompanied me to the brig. They'd brought four guards to deal with me. I was flattered.

When I looked at Sponder and his bleeding nose, I was pleased. The fucker.

I didn't say anything. Talking now wasn't the time. I'd humiliated Sponder enough. Doing anything now in front of Gaius would be foolish. I had no idea how Sponder had pulled a commissioner in to help with his cause to see me demoted to a trawler hauler.

And why? I hated the guy, but once I'd gotten reassigned to Starfighter MCS, I hadn't wanted to think of him again. Yet he kept coming back. He'd shown up here on the *Resolution* not once, but twice to deal with me personally.

Jennix had to know something was up.

But the mission was huge. Any petty fuckery Sponder had against me was nothing compared to the constant threat of IPBMs blowing up Velerion or any of our outposts. Jennix was focused on that. Not me.

I wasn't worried about myself. I was worried about Mia. She'd accepted her role as Starfighter MCS, *and* she'd accepted me as her pair bond. Now, because of Sponder's shit, she was going on a mission without me.

It was my fault. My guts that were hated. My choices that would now affect her.

She could die. Who was her partner for this mission? Was he or she qualified? As skilled as I was? Would they click and be able to work together as well as Mia and me?

Of course not.

And that was the motivation I needed to figure out how to get the hell out of the brig and onto the *Phantom.*

I might have broken Sponder's nose, but I wasn't going to fight the guard. I had no issue with him. He was doing his job. After we entered the prison area, there was only one on duty. He'd stood for the commissioner and escorted us down the short corridor. I counted two cells. Clearly the *Resolution* didn't have a lot of prisoners. I assumed any Dark Fleet captured would be taken elsewhere. This place was for those like me who were non-dangerous and would be transported to Velerion for a trial.

In fact, I'd expected to be taken with Gaius and Sponder off the *Resolution*, but once we were outside of the mission room, they'd argued.

"He should be taken to Velerion for immediate trial," Sponder had said to Gaius.

Gaius had disagreed. "The Starfighter is in custody, as you wanted. Jennix is correct. There is a mission to run that is critical to the survival of Velerion. *This* is not. He will remain here on the battleship until the mission is complete."

"But—" Sponder had sputtered.

"Your shuttle teams from Eos Station will be

without a leader, Captain. I expect you to focus on your job instead of this vendetta."

Vendetta?

Gaius had been right. Sponder had one against me. Sponder's hatred did not surprise me. However, his obsession with taking me down was a bit of a shock. I had expected him to be more than pleased to have me out of his way. To let me go. I had underestimated his need for vengeance, for control.

I had Gaius to thank for the small window of time he'd given me. I had to get out of here before Mia took off. I would not have her flying with some random Starfighter MCS. The person at her side would be me.

There would be serious consequences for my actions. Escape from jail after over fifty witnesses had watched my arrest wasn't smart. Jennix wouldn't be able to save me from this.

But I had to take care of Mia, and that was what mattered.

I rested for some time, waiting for an opportunity, dozing and watching for the guards to change shifts as I took in my surroundings. Noticed the panels covering the control system buried in the walls.

This wasn't my first time in the brig and I'd

learned a few tricks but I had to time my escape perfectly. Mia needed me, which meant I had to get to her before the mission started, but not so much of a window that I'd be caught and dragged back down here.

When the mission was just over an hour from launch, I took a deep breath.

"Guard!" I called. In this brig there were actual bars for the cell, unlike the laser beams that were used for the high-level prison on Velerion.

The guard came from his desk by the entrance. He was new to serve, perhaps only eighteen or nineteen years of age. "Your first post?" I asked.

He nodded.

"Must be boring."

The corner of his mouth tipped up. "You're the first prisoner we've had since I was assigned."

"Someone on duty at all times?"

"No, I'm part of the mechanic crew, but assigned as guard crew *per diem*."

"You're on call for when a prisoner comes in."

"Right. Like you. What did you do to get thrown in here?" He eyed me a little warily, as if I'd gone on a murdering spree.

"I pissed off an old commanding officer."

"They put you in here for that? Was it so bad a commissioner had to come from Velerion?"

"Yup." I sighed.

"Well, tough luck, but I have to get back to my team before launch."

"You'll just leave me?" I asked, faking concern.

"Yes, but the electronic controls will monitor your well-being."

I glanced around. "Electronic controls?"

He smiled. Pointed to the wall. "The system is state-of-the-art for a battleship. The monitors connect directly to the ship's central command station. You'll be monitored from there."

This kid was cool. A tech geek like me.

"Before you go, think you can get me something to eat? I don't want to be forgotten because of the mission."

"Sure."

He disappeared for a few minutes and then came back with a tray filled with standard food rations. It wasn't fancy, but it would do. He opened the small access door in the bars and passed me the tray.

"Thanks. Good luck with the mission."

"Fuck Queen Raya," he said before turning on his heel and leaving me behind.

Under the electronic controls of the system.

I ate as quickly as possible—because I was hungry and would need sustenance when I flew with Mia—and then set the tray on the bed. I picked up the knife. It was dull and probably wouldn't even pierce someone's skin, but it would work. The walls and ceiling were a smooth white. The floor had a glossy dark finish that matched the rest of the battleship.

There would be a control panel under one of these floor tiles that activated the locks on my prison cell's bars. That activated and controlled everything in this area. I needed to find it and hack into the locks to get the hell out of here and back to Mia.

I'd hacked the *Starfighter Training Academy.* I could hack this.

Almost an hour later, I did. The cell door opened, and I took off at a run. I had to hope I'd get to the docking bay in time to meet Mia before she took off.

Fortunately the entire battleship was in launch prep mode. I wasn't the only one running. When I got to the docking bay, I slowed. None of the ships had left yet. But the mechs were either walking away from their craft or doing the final steps on their checklists.

I went to the prep rooms where the flight suits

were kept and grabbed mine, changed into it in record time. I activated my retractable helmet to hide my face as I jogged to the *Phantom,* went up the ramp.

Mia and some asshole I'd never seen before were going through flight pre-checks.

"You're in my seat," I said.

Mia gasped and looked over her shoulder to see me. "What the hell? Kass?"

With a simple command I retracted my helmet so that it once again rested inside the flight suit's collar. "Pilot, I said you are in my seat."

The pilot looked confused but ready to argue. I couldn't blame him. I was willing to fight to sit next to the most talented, beautiful Starfighter MCS I'd ever met.

Rather than waste time arguing, I punched the pilot in the jaw, satisfied to see I hadn't lost my touch. He slumped in the seat, unconscious.

"Kass, what the hell are you doing?"

Unbuckling his flight harness took less than a second. Once he was loose, I yanked the pilot out of the chair, walked to the edge of the ramp, and rolled him down. "Hey, Mechs!" I yelled for Arria and Vintis, who came running.

"Is there a problem?" Arria asked. "Captain

Sponder was already down here with that commissioner, demanding to take a look at the ship. Said you might have done something to the system controls? Sabotaged it or something?"

"He's an asshole, and he's full of shit." I pointed to the unconscious pilot. "We had an extra passenger. Get him out of here and take him to medical, would you?"

"Sure thing." Vintis lifted the pilot over his shoulder with a grin and walked away. Once I knew we were clear, I waved to Arria, hit the button to close the ship up tight, and took my place next to my Mia.

Mia's jaw gaped, then closed, then opened again.

I leaned over and placed a hot, lingering kiss on those speechless lips. "Miss me?"

"What do you think you are doing?" She didn't sound like she'd missed me. She sounded angry.

I activated the launch sequence and buckled into my seat as the *Phantom* lifted from the floor of the launch bay. "You didn't really believe I was going to let you go out there all alone, did you?"

"I wasn't alone."

"Yes, love, you were."

Mia didn't argue, and I took that as a good sign. I

jumped on the opportunity to speak my truth to the only person whose opinion of me mattered.

"Mia, I hacked into the training program because Sponder refused to approve my application to the Starfighter program, despite the fact that I was more than qualified. But that's all I did. I am not a cheater or a liar, not about things that matter. Every training mission we ran together, we completed. You are my pair bond, and I am not giving you up. I don't give a fuck what Sponder claims. When we get back from this mission, I'll find a way to prove my innocence and destroy that asshole's career, for good this time."

"This time?"

We shot out into space, and I turned the *Phantom* toward Xenon. "Long story."

"We have time."

No, we didn't. We were heading into battle, and I did not want to spend the entire time talking about that fucker, but... "Arria said the commissioner and Sponder were down here, looking at the ship?"

Mia nodded, her mind clearly beginning to focus on the mission. "Sponder was actually on board when I arrived to meet the pilot you just punched out."

I grinned. "Don't remember his name, do you?"

Finally she smiled. "No. Is that a bad thing?"

"Not to me." I tried to think of any reason that Sponder would be on our ship, and came up with nothing.

"Was Commissioner Gaius with him?"

"Sponder? No. He was alone when I got here, but the mechs saw the Commissioner here. He must have been gone by that time I arrived."

Mia turned away from me, her attention completely focused on her screens. Which was fine with me. I didn't want to talk about Sponder or Gaius or cheating, and I didn't want Mia upset right before such a critical mission.

But once this mission was over? Things with Sponder were going critical, and I had no intention of losing that battle.

This time, I wouldn't hesitate to take the fucker down.

10

ℳia, *The* Phantom

XENON ALPHA, the moon filling our view screens, was beautiful. Unlike Earth's moon, this one rippled in waves of reds, oranges, and browns, more like Saturn than the bare rock I was used to, Earth's moon was always glowing silver with darker craters. I had no idea what this one looked like from Xenon itself, but the dark black spot we were heading toward reminded me, not of the caterpillar I'd imagined in the briefing, but now a black leech sucking the moon's blood. I had no idea where that creepy image had come from, but I didn't like this place. It felt... wrong.

"How long until we're in range?" I asked.

"An hour, give or take." Kass sat at the pilot's controls as I monitored every bit of energy, frequency, or light approaching or leaving the moon. His presence, while I was still upset with him, somehow helped me breathe. The last mission had been exciting, a chance to prove our skills, a wild ride in outer space with no one at risk but ourselves.

This was completely different. Fighting squadrons from the *Battleship Resolution* were on standby waiting for us to take down the odd magnetic field being generated on this moon. Starfighters. Shuttle pilots. Titan teams. And the people on Xenon, their entire population was less than the number of people who lived in one suburb of Berlin.

Not a lot of people by planetary standards. But when every life on that planet depended on one Starfighter MCS team to liberate them from Dark Fleet control? Depended on *me?*

Kass and I were literally the *only* MCS team they had. We were alone out here. Truly alone. I felt like I was breaking an entire city full of innocent people out of a maximum-security prison, and if I messed this up, they might all die. Thousands and thousands of prisoners, dead with the push of a button.

Did they have those zapper collars on their necks like some of the freakish science fiction movies? Did Queen Raya have a big red button on her throne, one push and everyone's heads would explode?

"I don't like this." Normally I would have kept the thought to myself, but this was Kass. After all the missions we'd done together in the game, he wasn't going to ignore my instincts.

"We're almost there," he replied.

Our comms lit up, and I looked at Kass, held his gaze as I answered. "MCS Becker."

"*Phantom,* this is Group Five Leader."

Oh hell. General Jennix.

"Copy that, Group Leader. Go ahead."

"Commissioner Gaius's prisoner escaped from the brig prior to mission launch. We have unconfirmed reports that there is a pilot in medical claiming to have seen him on board the *Phantom* prior to launch. Can you confirm?"

"I don't know what you're talking about, General."

"I see." There was a long pause, and I waited, watching Kass. He clenched his jaw, then reached down to his controls and activated his comm.

"General, this is MCS Remeas. I was unable to allow MCS Becker, my pair bond, to go into battle alone, sir. I will turn myself in once we return to base."

"MCS Becker, are you all right? Are you able to complete the mission?"

"Affirmative. The mission is a go," I said.

"Very well. I will deal with both of you after this is done. Jennix out."

I bit my lower lip as I turned my entire focus, my existence to the screens and code in front of me. And then... I couldn't hold my tongue a moment longer. "Kass?"

"Yes, love."

Damn it, why did he have to call me that when I was ready to rip his head from his body and shove it down his throat for lying to me. For humiliating me. For making me doubt everything and everyone, including myself.

"I hacked into the training program," I admitted. All I'd been feeling for him had been anger, but my voice was quiet now. Almost... done in. "I saw the evidence myself. Every single mission we completed had been tampered with. Why did you do that?"

"What are you talking about?" He turned in his seat to stare at me. Eyes wide, stunned. He didn't have an easy way about him. He was uncomfortable.

Angry. Off-kilter, which was a new and unusual look from him.

"I hacked into the *Starfighter Training Academy* system. I pulled up our training records. Every single mission we completed—every single one, Kass—had been modified to make the tasks easier to complete."

He shook his head in complete denial. "No."

"Why did you do that?" I would ask the same question over and over until he answered me.

He swallowed hard, stared at me until he was sure I was looking—or mesmerized. "I vow to you, bonded one, I did no such thing. If I were going to cheat the system, do you really think I would be stupid enough, or sloppy enough, to leave that obvious a trail?"

I took a moment to consider that. I'd hacked into that program in less than an hour. I'd found the data I was looking for within minutes once I was in. I could have just as easily deleted the mission modifications and erased my digital footprint. It would have been simple to complete. I could have erased everything, cleared Kass's name, and Sponder would have nothing to go on. Kass would have been proven innocent. Guaranteed.

If I could make him look innocent in less than

ten minutes, it made sense that someone else could make him look guilty just as easily.

Why hadn't I thought of that while I'd been in there?

Because I was being emotional, not logical. I'd doubted myself from the start. All Captain Sponder had to do was wave a red flag in front of me and I'd charged like the proverbial bull. Hurt. Angry. Betrayed.

Poor little Mia, lied to again.

Not good enough.

Bad judgment.

Shit. I'd let that asshole Sponder lead me around by the nose like a naive first-year recruit. All because my heart was involved. Because when it came to Kass, there was no logic for me. Because I'd believed in Sponder over Kass. God, I loved him. I wanted him. And I wanted him to believe in me so much it terrified me. The first chance to jump ship and I'd taken it.

No more.

"Mia?"

I looked at Kass with new eyes. "You are telling the truth."

He sighed. His shoulders relaxed. All the tension left his body.

"Yes." The unspoken *DUH* wasn't said aloud, but I could see it in his eyes. Along with the hurt I'd caused by doubting him. And myself.

"Why does Sponder hate you so much?" I asked finally.

Kass sighed and turned away from me to check the ship's controls. "He's an ass. He's always been an ass. Once, he harassed a female shuttle pilot. A friend of mine. He physically assaulted her. She fought him off, reported the incident. Nothing happened. Commissioner Gaius is his uncle."

"Uncle Gaius saved him?" So Sponder was a silver spoon who hadn't earned his rank or his pilots' respect.

"He got a slap on the wrist, and she got written up for disobeying a senior officer. He was making her life a living hell after that, so I hacked into the system, downloaded the video files of his attack from the top-level security feed, stashed them away, and transferred her to another base, as far away from him as I could get her."

I widened my eyes at all he'd done for a friend. "And he knew you did it?"

He shrugged. "Well, the transfer order was in his name, but he knew it was me. I told him. He wanted her back under his control. He was totally obsessed.

When he tried to have her returned to Eos Station, I went to his office, told him I had video of his attack, and that if he went near her again, I'd ruin his career."

"Why are you still under his command? When was this?"

Kass chuckled. "Right before he denied my application and I had to hack into the *Starfighter Training Academy* program. About a year ago."

"Why didn't you leave? Ask for a transfer? Or transfer yourself out like you did your friend?"

"He hates me, but he couldn't touch me, not when I had the video evidence to ruin him and his uncle since he was the one who made it go away. There were too many other vulnerable new recruits under his command that might have been next."

"So, you watched over the sheep."

"What is a sheep?" He frowned.

"Never mind. I believe you. But that's not enough. Not for this. He's hated you for a year but never tried to have you locked up before. He somehow hacked into the system and modified our training data. What do you think set him off?"

Kass stared into the dark emptiness of space for long minutes. "I don't know. Maybe the audit we brought down on him? Maybe he's afraid that if the tech and security teams go digging into his records, they'll find out what an ass he is."

"Maybe." I casually monitored the data streams coming from Xenon Alpha as I allowed my mind to wander. With his uncle a Velerion commissioner, I doubted Sponder was too worried about Kass taking him down. So, was he worried about the audit General Jennix had threatened him with? Was he hoping that by framing Kass, the audit would be canceled? Or maybe that his uncle would be able to pull some strings, have the audit canceled, and the general would have no reason to protest?

Something didn't add up. Just like I'd thought earlier in our quarters.

I linked the *Phantom's* data stream back to *Battleship Resolution* and waited as the much more powerful battleship's comm system synced with Velerion and the Hall of Records.

Captain Sponder was hiding something, and I was going to find out what that something was.

For the first time I felt my cipher implants working alongside my mind, speeding up the transfer of information, making it easier for me to communicate with the ship. I took a moment to adjust, to become accustomed to the *feel* of it, like my brain had become wireless and connected directly to the data streams. For a moment I couldn't move, shocked by the ease of the data transfer and the speed of information moving through my mind. But I was also grateful. I had a *lot* of records to search and not a lot of time to do it.

Kass was quiet as I worked.

Fifteen minutes later I froze in my chair. I had it. I fucking had the proof we needed to take Sponder down. "Kass, who is Delegate Rainhart?"

Kass scoffed. "A traitor. Your friend Jamie and her pair bond, Alex, found out recently that he was the one who gave Queen Raya the details about the Starfighter base that had been destroyed. He betrayed Velerion and gave the Dark Fleet exactly what they needed to wipe out almost all our Starfighters and cripple Velerion's defenses."

Oh shit.

"What's a delegate?"

"They are appointed by the commissioners. Kind of like Graves to General Jennix. They work for the commissioners as trusted appointees to negotiate, meet with constituents and merchants, take care of a lot of the day-to-day responsibilities of the commissioners who are elected to the Hall of Records."

"Like their chief of staff?"

"I am not familiar with that office."

"How long do we have?" I was anxious, the adrenaline flowing after a puzzle like this had been solved. We had the answer, and we had to do something about it. Now.

"Five minutes, tops. Find anything good on Sponder yet?"

"As a matter of fact, I—"

BOOM!

"Mia! Hold on!" Kass's shout accompanied the *Phantom* rotating suddenly. I was strapped into my seat, but even in space, inertia was real and my head was thrown back.

"What the hell?" I shouted as an unnatural flare of heat washed over me. The control station in front of me caught fire and was immediately put out by the fire suppression system.

"Kass?"

"Rebooting the system," Kass replied, his voice even.

Within seconds I had my screens back and everything looked normal. "What was that?"

"I don't know."

"Anything on scanners?" I asked, my gaze roving over everything in sight looking for enemy ships or anything that could have been the source of the attack.

"No."

That made no sense. The ship rattled around us, shaking like we were in the middle of an earthquake. I checked my monitors and could not believe what I was seeing. "Kass, the entire right side of the *Phantom* is gone."

"I know."

He knew? "Were we hit?"

"Not from the outside."

"What?" Alarms filled the small cabin, and the ship's emergency power system took over, shutting down my station completely and funneling all emergency power to Kass's flight controls. My flight suit responded to the ship's ping, my helmet rising to cover my head.

The control panel in front of me jumped and rattled, forcing my gloved hands to lift.

"I can't get my hands on the controls."

"Hold on!"

A screeching like nothing I'd ever heard filled the cockpit. Two heartbeats after my helmet locked in place, the panel above my head was torn off by passing debris and the atmosphere was sucked out of the cockpit. "Kass? You okay?"

"I'm fine. But someone put a bomb on this ship. And we both know who."

I looked up, out of where the ceiling of the cockpit should have been, and saw nothing but empty space. And stars. Spinning stars.

"We're spinning."

"We are." Kass's voice was calm but stressed. "Just like the training mission on Gamma 479 where we lost a wing."

Right. We'd been through this before. *Breathe.* "You got this?"

I wasn't on my couch in front of my TV. We were in space. This crash was actually going to hurt, if we survived at all.

"I'll get us on the ground, but we're going to have to hack the moon base's system from the inside. That bomb took out our long-range comms."

And our ability to fly. My ability to do my job.

"Great." I braced myself in the copilot's seat and moved it back into position next to Kass. I had to tell him now. Had to. Just in case. "I'm sorry, Kass. I'm sorry I doubted you."

He flicked his gaze to me. "You believe me now?"

"Yes. I do." I took a deep breath and said the words I could never take back. "I love you, Kassius Remeas. I love you."

His eyes flared, his jaw clenched. "You tell me now?"

I couldn't help the sly smile. "Yeah, so don't get us killed. Okay?"

He chuckled. "Copy that, bonded one."

Even now, tense and scared and nervous, that voice grounded me.

Kass fought the ship for control as the oddly beautiful moon grew larger and larger on his screen. I thought we were going to make it, I really did, until the cannons mounted on the moon base suddenly came to life and pointed straight at us.

"Oh shit. Kass?"

"Incoming! Brace!" he shouted.

Bright light shot from the cannons, and Kass somehow, by luck or skill or divine intervention, managed to take the *Phantom* low enough to the ground that the weapons' fire blasted overhead like strobe lights above the open top of the ship.

The rattling inside my head was painful as Kass turned the *Phantom* onto her side for a rough landing. We hit rock. Hard.

Heavy bolts held my chair in place as equipment was ripped from beneath my fingers and hurtled away from the ship.

"Fuck! Hold on!" Kass needn't have bothered yelling the order. I was already holding on to the thick straps that crossed my chest, the only thing I could reach. My feet dangled before me, open space all that I could see as our ship bounced on the rough surface and finally slid to a halt. The *Phantom* was on her side, my half of the ship open, almost completely gone.

"Mia?" Before I'd registered the stop, Kass was reaching for me with fumbling fingers. He released the harness and pulled me out of the seat and into his arms. "Are you hurt?"

I took stock. Rattled? Yes. Hurt? "No. I'm fine." I wrapped my arms around him and squeezed for long seconds as I fought to control my frantic breathing. "What... what just happened?"

"The bomb blew our stealth actions and comms. The moon base's defense system saw us coming and shot us down."

I was shaking. So I wasn't bleeding, but I was rattled. Big-time. "You really think Sponder planted a bomb on our ship?"

Kass shook his head. "It's the only explanation."

I rested against his chest, gave myself permission to breathe for at least a minute. "Why would he do that? You weren't even on the ship. You were locked up in the brig."

"You were not," he countered, his voice grim.

"The only way he can truly hurt me, Mia, is by hurting you. He knows that."

"That's crazy. And not true." I'd told him I loved him, and he had *not* said it back. Yes, he'd been busy trying to save our lives at the time, but still, a woman had needs.

"It is, my Mia. Without you, I'm nothing. I have no home, no family. I have the fleet and I have you. Ask me which one matters more."

Damn it, I took the bait. "Which one matters more?"

His eyes met mine. Held. "You, love. I love you, too."

Ahhh. Everything inside me melted, and I allowed the feeling to flood me. I deserved this moment. We both did. "I wish I could take this helmet off and kiss you."

Kass squeezed me tightly. "When we get these suits off, I'm going to do a lot more than kiss you."

"I'm going to hold you to that."

"I don't lie, remember."

By tacit agreement, we turned to inspect our options for an exit from the wreckage.

"We can crawl through there." I pointed to a particularly large hole near the rear of the ship.

"Yes." Kass reached behind me and pulled a

portable mission kit from a large cabinet that, luckily, was still in one piece. Inside the case would be the equipment we would need to hack into the base's automated system, sync with it, and shut it down.

I wasn't used to doing this away from a computer, but I could do an on-site job. I'd just never imagined doing it on a moon.

Kass took my hand and helped pull me through the opening to stand on the moon's hard surface. It was like walking on top of a cast-iron skillet, except red, not black.

I stomped my boot and regretted it as the reactionary force sent me into a jump high enough that I could have kicked Kass in the chest without trying. I landed with a soft *thud*. Awesome. "This moon is hard as a rock."

"It *is* a rock."

That made me smile as the ship was struck by laser cannon fire. The weapon was mounted on the base. We ducked and ran low to the ground as the base's automated system continued to fire on what was left of our beautiful ship. The abandoned moon base looked like a giant leech from the ground, too. Oblong and segmented like a worm, the ends tapered toward the moon's surface, perhaps even tunneling below.

"Why is this base so ugly?"

"The Velerion engineers were not concerned with aesthetics. The shell-like structure can be retracted in sections as needed, and the curved armor is more effective against random space debris. A straight wall would take more damage. With this, much of the impact forces can be partially redirected."

We were halfway to the nearest segmented piece of curved wall when our ship exploded. Must have been the fuel tanks. Nothing left but a shell. A burned, crispy shell. "Ashes to ashes and dust to dust, *Phantom.* You were a good ship," I said. Now we were stuck on the moon.

"We'll get another one," Kass said, pulling me along behind him.

"I'm calling the next one *Bad Bitch* so no one will fuck with her."

I heard Kass's smile in his voice. "That is a horrible name for a ship. You named the *Phantom.* I think I should name the next one."

We ran into the side of the base and leaned against the smooth wall to catch our breaths. "Oh yeah? And what would you name her?" I checked my oxygen readings and closed my eyes in relief when they read normal. The suits had complex life support systems built into the lining, as well as all kinds of data I didn't understand moving across the visor. I was not a biochemist. In the game, these space suits would keep the player alive for several days with complex recycling technology. I had to hope that was actually true in real life as well. And I wasn't going to ask. If that was *not* the case, I did *not* want to know.

"I was thinking I would name her after your favorite thing in the universe." Kass turned toward the wall and withdrew a small cutting torch from somewhere. He was a space Boy Scout. He had a hole big enough to crawl through about half-done when I surrendered to curiosity, despite my better judgment, and decided to take the bait.

"We can't name our new ship Kassius."

He laughed but kept focused on his task. "I knew you loved me."

So, he was funny and cavalier and charming, and totally distracting me from the thought that we were going to die on this stupid moon. "All right, I'll bite. What is my favorite thing in the universe?"

Finished cutting, he kicked a hole in the wall, and the thick piece he'd cut clattered to rest inside the dark interior of the base.

"Justice."

11

I TURNED off the laser torch and capped it before shoving the handheld device back into its holster at my hip. Mia stood with her back braced against the base wall when I kicked in the outer shell to grant us access.

She'd said I was her favorite thing in the universe.

"Justice. I like it." Mia held her pistol at the ready, watching my back. There was no need. At least, not yet. The base was unmanned and automated, but the explosion on our ship would have alerted the Dark Fleet's security network to our presence. As long as we didn't stand in front of a laser cannon and beg the thing to shoot us, we should be fine. The base's defenses were made to take down ships, not individuals on foot.

Still, that was dated information. No one from Velerion had set foot on this moon since the Dark Fleet had attacked Xenon and turned the colonists into factory slaves. We hadn't planned on setting foot on it either, but plans changed.

I swung the equipment bag's strap off my shoulder and settled the heavy bulk just inside the opening I'd cut. Stepping in first to make sure there were no hidden weapons within, I motioned for Mia to join me inside. As she took my hand and stepped over the remains of the lower wall, I worked on setting up the portable comm unit. "We need to let Jennix know we're not dead."

"Good idea."

Once set up, I activated the comm unit, even though I was probably painting a target on our backs if the Dark Fleet scanned the area. "Group Five Leader, this is MCS One; come in."

"This is Group Five Leader. Go ahead."

"We lost the *Phantom,* but the mission is on target. We are inside the base."

"Thank Vega." I couldn't miss the relief in her

voice. "Notify us when you are ready for retrieval. I will alert Group Two. We will monitor the force field from here."

"Copy that."

"And Starfighters?"

I stilled inside. The general had called me a Starfighter, despite the fact that I was supposed to be rotting in a prison cell right now. She was on our side. Once I told her everything, I had no doubt she would help me take down Sponder.

"Yes, General?"

"We're all glad we haven't lost you. Stay alert and stay safe."

"Copy that. MCS One out."

That done, I crouched down and helped Mia set out the rest of our equipment on the smooth, cold floor. Everything inside the base was the same matte black as the exterior. Dull. Boring. The base looked like a dark cancerous blight from space, if one knew where to look.

Mia sat with her back to the wall and our hacking equipment splayed out across her lap. I took the communication and sensors and set up my small operations center. Once the scanners were finished, I breathed a sigh of relief. We were alone, at least at the moment. If Queen Raya had soldiers stationed inside, they weren't being picked up by our scanners.

"All clear?" she asked, most likely thinking the same thing.

"So far. How long do you need?"

She shrugged. "I don't know. I've never done this before."

She cleared her throat, and I looked at her. "What is it?"

"Why didn't you tell the general about Sponder?"

"Over the open comm channel? No. I don't want him to have a chance to run."

"Okay." She was distracted, her gaze already darting at lightning speed from screen to screen on her display, her fingers racing over the controls.

"Besides, we've got more important things to deal with. Tell me the moment you break through, or..." My voice trailed off, but I didn't need to finish the thought.

"Or there will be nothing left of us by the time anyone shows up to give us a ride?"

"Exactly."

One of my scanners beeped, and I glanced down. "Oh fuck."

Mia's hands never stopped moving as she settled into her task. "What is it?"

I debated not telling her the truth for all of ten seconds until she stopped and looked at me. Really *looked.*

"Kass?"

Fuck. Even through the shielded visor her brown eyes were beautiful. How could I tell her we were about to die?

Mia tilted her head, her gaze narrowing. "Kass, tell me what the hell is happening. Right now."

I sighed. I loved this woman, could keep nothing from her. "The base's automated system just sent an alert to Xandrax."

"Queen Raya's planet? What does that mean?"

"Four minutes for the signal to get there. Two or three minutes for them to decide to blow this place to pieces. Four minutes for the order to come back."

Her eyes widened as she did the math. "So, we're either off this rock or dead in the next ten minutes?"

"At the most."

"*Scheisse.*"

Our gazes met, held. "What do you want to do? I can call in for a ride now. Get us out of here."

Mia didn't move as she considered our options. "Do it, but I'm not leaving until we do our job. If we don't take down the shield generator on this base, the entire mission will fail. All those people down there will still be under Raya's control and the IPBMs will still be a threat. I can't live with that."

"Mia, I can't live without you." I couldn't accept this fate for us. Wouldn't. "I'm calling it in, letting them know we need to lift off in six minutes. If you aren't finished, I will throw you over my shoulder and carry you onto that shuttle."

"Six minutes is an eternity."

"Stop talking and get to work. Six minutes."

Mia lowered her head and focused on the task of breaking into the moon base's operational system as I set a timer sequence in my visor. Worst-case scenario, we'd have to run at eight minutes and put as much distance between us and the base as possible, hope the bomb or missile Queen Raya sent to destroy this place was small, and pray the shuttle pilot Group Two sent to retrieve us was good. Really fucking good.

I waited. Impatiently. I trusted my pair bond to do her job. Yet, fuck... the clock was ticking. Two minutes, twenty-seven seconds of silence.

"I'm in." Mia's words made my heart speed its pace. Just a little. "Time?"

"Two twenty-seven."

"Okay. I've got this."

A minute passed.

Another.

"Mia?"

"Don't talk to me."

Fuck.

I couldn't remain silent. "We just hit five minutes."

"The encryption code is like nothing I've ever seen."

"Ninety seconds and we're out of here."

"No. I'm almost there. I have an idea. It's a long shot, but—"

"Eighty. Seventy-nine. Seventy-eight."

"Stop talking."

"Mia. I will drag your ass out of here."

"Not yet."

Fuck. Fuck. Fuck. My scanners flashed bright warning lights. It was what I feared: a bioflare warhead was headed for our location. Bad news? The weapon would turn anything organic into a pile of ash, but the base would remain intact, the shielding on, the Dark Fleet protected. The good news was we had just over a minute longer than I'd estimated. "Incoming."

"Call for that ride," she said.

Thank fuck. I stood and activated my comms.

"Group Five Leader, this is MCS One requesting emergency evac."

"MCS One, this is command. We are tracking a bioflare heading in your direction. Impact in two minutes." General Jennix's voice sounded concerned but not surprised to discover Queen Raya was willing to sacrifice any men she had on this moon base in order to take us out.

"Yes, General. We are aware. We're in. We'll have the shield down in—" I glanced at Mia.

"Now."

"Now, General. The shield should be deactivating now."

"Excellent."

"Requesting emergency evac at this location." I shared my location data with the Velerion fleet as Mia rose to stand next to me.

"Copy that. Passing you to Group Two. I notified them of your situation. They should have a shuttle standing by."

Team Two was the shuttle teams under the command of Captain Sponder. How ironic that the asshole who'd tried to kill us was going to have to save our lives. One of the shuttles had to be close enough to swoop down and pick us up. That had been part of the plan, a contingency in case anything had gone wrong. A last resort option in case Mia got into trouble. I was supposed to be in the brig right now, but Mia was a Starfighter MCS. An asset that General Jennix would find nearly impossible to replace. We'd learned the value of our Starfighter teams the hard way, when we'd lost them in Queen Raya's sneak attack.

"This is Group Two. Go ahead."

"This is Starfighter MCS *Phantom* requesting emergency evac. We have ninety seconds to impact."

I expected a quick, efficient response. Instead I heard a monotone voice I recognized all too well, Captain Sponder. "Starfighter MCS Remeas?"

"Affirmative."

"This is Team Two Leader. When we lost contact with the *Phantom,* the moon base shuttle team was reassigned to medical evac. I do not have a ship in place to reach you in time, *Phantom.* Estimated arrival of nearest shuttle team is seven minutes. Bioflare impact would take out any approaching shuttles. I can't send a team in. It's too dangerous."

"What?" Mia's gasp made me wince with guilt. If it weren't for me, Captain Sponder, the leader of Group Two, would have done what he was supposed to do. A shuttle would have been standing by, close enough to get here in under a minute, as the mission parameters required, regardless of whether or not our ship had gone down. Instead he was going to make up some fuck-all excuse, no one would be able to prove he'd done anything wrong, all evidence of the bomb he'd planted on Mia's ship would be destroyed and Mia would be dead.

Fuck.

Of course, he'd planned on her being dead already.

There was no time to argue. No other group would have a ship in place to assist. That responsibility had been assigned to Group Two. Sponder's group.

"We have to run, Mia!"

"Shit. He knows I know. He really did want me dead all along." She stood, abandoning her equipment. We would sprint, run as fast as we could, but it wasn't going to be fast enough.

"Yeah, and for me to suffer knowing you are going to die. Come on." I took Mia's hand and pulled her out of the moon base and onto the surface.

"There's nowhere to run, Kass."

I scanned the horizon, desperate for a rocky outcropping, a groove in the ground, anywhere that would give us the slightest chance of survival. "Run for the ship."

Hand in hand we sprinted across the moon's surface toward the remains of our ship. Perhaps, if we could hide behind the wreckage, maybe even burrow inside somewhere behind the hull, we would survive the bioflare coming for us.

Mia tugged her hand free of mine and pulled ahead, increasing our pace. I followed, unwilling to run ahead of her. If we were going to die, I would die shielding Mia.

"I know this isn't the best time..." Mia panted the words as we ran for our lives.

"I'm here."

"It's crazy. And stupid. And makes no sense. But I love you. If I'm going to die, I'm glad it's with you. I have no regrets, Kass. I want you to know that."

Her breathing was ragged as we sprinted.

"I love you, Mia. And I'm sorry. I'm so fucking sorry. Sponder's not sending someone because of me." My visor's alert system flashed a warning, and I glanced into space. "There it is."

Mia looked up as well, and I knew exactly what made her gasp. The bioflare was clearly visible, its comet-like tail leaving a trail of brilliant blue light streaking behind it. "Oh shit."

"Keep moving."

"We're not going to make it." Mia ran despite her

dire prediction. "And it's not because of you. He's working with Delegate Rainhart. Sponder. He's a traitor, and he was afraid I was going to figure it out."

"What?" I stumbled and nearly fell. "No, Mia. What are you saying?"

Her words came in bursts as she fought for breath. "Sponder. He's been working with Rainhart for at least three years. Since before the original Starfighter base was attacked. He's a traitor. He was nervous when Jennix threatened him with that audit, but after today he knows I know."

My mind scrambled, trying to make sense of what she was telling me. "How would he know that?"

Twenty-five seconds and the *Phantom* was still at least thirty paces away.

"I sort of sent some information to General Jennix on the way here."

Twenty seconds.

"Mia, why didn't you tell—"

A blast of light rose over the moon's horizon from just ahead of us. A starfighter. "Would you two stop chatting and get your asses over here before we all blow the fuck up."

Mia laughed out loud as I tried to register where I'd heard that female voice before.

"Jamie? Did you just say 'fuck'?" Mia asked between gasps of air.

That was Jamie and Alexius?

"Yes. So get your asses over here. I like my ship almost as much as I like you. Don't make me choose."

A small starfighter moved close, then hovered just above the ground, almost far enough away to be safely out of range of the bioflare. Almost. Neither Mia nor I slowed our pacing as a small door opened on the side. There was no ramp, just Alexius reaching his arm out toward us.

Mia reached up first, and Alexius pulled her inside as I followed, leaping behind her. Alexius made sure I was secure before slamming the door closed and squeezing past us. It was tight, but I held Mia against my chest as Alexius slipped behind her, back to the copilot's seat. There were two jump seats behind them, facing one another, with just enough room that Mia and I might not rub our knees together.

I tugged Mia to the seats, and we sat immediately.

"Buckle up. This might get bumpy."

"Five seconds," I said, checking the time. Fuck.

"Hold on!" Jamie shouted the warning as their

ship took off like a beam of light, racing away from the moon's surface.

I watched the countdown in my visor.

Four.

Three.

Two.

One.

The ship bucked and jolted like we were tumbling down a rocky cliff. Somehow Jamie and Alexius kept the ship under control. Its outer hull shielded us from the worst of the blast, the temperature rising inside their starfighter just enough to make me uncomfortable. But our skin hadn't melted off our bodies, so I considered that a win.

I only had one side of my harness buckled. Mia was less fortunate, her body swinging wildly as she hung on to the shoulder straps with her gloved hands. Once we stabilized, I reached for her leg and pulled her back down into her seat. She buckled the harness with shaking fingers as I held her in place.

"Thanks." She grinned at me, and I sighed with relief. She was unharmed. Thank Vega.

"Anytime, my Mia."

A voice came through the starfighter's ship comm. "Starfighters? This is General Jennix on a secure channel."

"Yes, General," Jamie responded.

"Confirm retrieval of the Starfighter MCS pair."

Jamie looked over her shoulder at me. Mia sat directly behind her, so the two Earth women could not make eye contact. Instead Jamie reached back with her hand, which Mia gripped at once.

"Affirmative."

"Excellent news, Starfighter. Return them to the *Resolution,* then continue with your original mission. I have informed General Aryk of your detour, but you are to say nothing. The shuttle teams are now directly under General Aryk's command. As far as Captain Sponder is concerned, Mia and Kassius are dead."

I looked to Mia. She eyed me.

"Yes, General." Jamie ended the comm and the four of us sat in silence for a few seconds. The quiet did nothing to dampen the cold rage settling like an ice blanket over my bones.

"He almost killed you," I said. "Not once but twice." I'd hated Sponder before, but now... he'd wanted Mia dead. Me? I knew he had it in for me, but nothing... *no one* fucked with my pair bond.

Before the bomb, it had been my mission to be free of Sponder. Now he was going down.

$\mathcal{M}$ ia

JAMIE AND ALEX flew the *Valor* back to *Battleship Reso-lution* with the comm channels open so we could all hear what was happening. When our ship exploded, the mission had been paused. All teams had been battle ready and waiting for the shields to go down to begin their portion of the takeover of Xenon. But the entire plan hinged on Kass and me overriding the controls on the moon base. No one—ourselves included—expected to do it by hand. On the moon's surface.

Or that we'd survived the crash. But our comms to General Jennix had kept the mission from being aborted or delayed. As soon as we'd shut down Dark Fleet control of the moon base, the mission was a *go*.

We'd survived. We'd taken down the force field around Xenon that the Dark Fleet was using to keep Velerion forces from regaining control of their colony and the factories. We'd done everything we were asked to do, and now our role was complete.

As Jamie took us back to the battleship, we heard the details of the rest of the mission. Everything. The attack. The losses. The way the people of Xenon rose up to help overthrow the ground forces under Queen Raya's command as well as the Dark Fleet ships serving her once the force field had been removed.

It was a quick assault. A quick victory. I could only imagine how eager the Xenon colonists were for their liberation.

Jamie and Alex didn't linger at the docking station, only hovering the *Valor* over it so we could descend the ramp before it was retracted. Then they were off.

So were we. Straight to the forward operations center inside the battleship's control room.

In all the years I'd worked in law enforcement, helped to hunt down and capture the bad guys, I'd never wanted to see anyone behind bars as much as

Sponder. I'd met people who were vile. Evil. Without conscience. But I'd never hated any of them.

I hated Captain Sponder.

I was possessive of Kass. Ridiculously so. Knowing that Sponder had it in for Kass, that he'd almost kept him away from me, made me furious. But knowing Sponder had actually planted evidence to see him rot in jail for something he didn't do, made me clench my fists, ready to break his nose all over again. And Kass was just the tip of the iceberg. I didn't know much about what had happened to the Velerion people over the last two or three years, but Sponder had probably killed thousands of people. Thousands. He was pure evil.

But Kass? He was so far past where I was in his anger. His jaw was clenched, his face a hard mask. He had a mission of his own. Nothing, not even Commissioner Gaius, was going to stop him this time. Uncle or no uncle, Sponder was finished.

We made our way through the maze of corridors to get to the forward operations command center, our pace swift. The doors slid silently open, but the room was full of commotion and noise. It looked like the Houston NASA control room in the movies. A front wall was covered in comms screens, each one showing a different part of the mission. Ground fighters. Air battles. Everything was happening at once. This was the place where it could all be witnessed simultaneously.

And everyone was going to see what happened next.

Kass stopped just inside the entry. His gaze scanned the room until he locked on, like an IPBM targeting a planet, to Sponder, who was onboard the *Resolution* and sitting at his command station like the cat who ate the canary. He thought we were dead. He believed his treachery had gone undetected. Again.

Kass stalked around the rows of control desks and stopped beside the man. Sponder looked up, his eyes widening, and he stood. In fact he hopped up much faster than I expected for someone of his age.

"You belong in the brig," Sponder said. His nose was crooked and swollen, and he'd have two black eyes in a few hours from Kass's earlier headbutt.

"You belong in the ground."

The mission continued around us, but Jennix came over. Another general—I assumed since the uniforms matched—as well.

"MCS, this is not the time," Jennix said.

Kass took a second but finally lifted his gaze from Sponder. He looked over the asshole's shoulder at Jennix.

"It is, General. He locked me up with fabricated evidence, planted a bomb on the *Phantom,* which not only was intended to jeopardize the entire mission, but murder Mia and the other pilot. And he refused to retrieve us from the moon surface in order to cover his crimes."

As Kass spoke, Sponder started to sputter and deny.

"Who knows what other ways he's sabotaged Velerion? Or this mission."

Jennix didn't even blink.

"Why should I trust the words of an MCS who cheated?" Jennix asked. She knew the truth. I could see it in her eyes, but she was enjoying watching Sponder squirm. As was I.

"Innocent until proven guilty, General," Kass replied.

She crossed her arms over her chest. "The same could be said for Sponder."

"I request his immediate removal from the command center!" Sponder said.

Jennix didn't even blink. I took the locked stare between Kass and the general as my cue. I made my way down to the trio, nodded to the new general— Aryk, I thought, because he was the one who'd been on Jamie's screen when she'd won the game.

I crossed my arms over my chest and let the hate boil through my blood. "Sponder is a traitor and a liar, General, and I found the proof," I said. "You have it. All of it. I sent it to you."

Sponder went quiet.

"And Sponder had the proof to have you arrested," Jennix said to Kass.

"I said I *found* the proof. *You* have it. I sent it to you before the *Phantom* exploded."

Jennix eyed me and continued to play her role. I had no idea why she was doing this, but I didn't question her choices. Perhaps she had to play this game to satisfy the Commissioner? Or to solidify mine and Kass's reputation as a highly skilled Starfighter MCS team.

"Graves!" she shouted.

"Yes, General." Her emissary appeared almost immediately.

"You are Group Five Leader until I return."

"Yes, General," Graves repeated, then disappeared.

"Comms," Jennix said to the room. "Retrieve Jennix data files sent from MCS Becker. Past two hours."

"Processing," the AI-generated voice replied. "Data visible on screen six."

Jennix pivoted on her heel and walked to a screen along the side wall and stood for long minutes, reading. Processing. She stared at the display. I knew when she read the details of Sponder's connection to Delegate Rainhart because her spine stiffened and I could almost see the steam coming off her shoulders. Her self-control was admirable, as was her acting skill.

"Explain, MCS Becker," she said.

"This is preposterous, General," Sponder sputtered, but a trickle of sweat ran down his cheek.

Jennix held up her hand. "The *Phantom* mysteriously exploded, Captain. I have questions. If Becker's data is inaccurate, she will share a cell with her pair bond."

Which meant she believed me—and the data I'd sent to her—because, if she didn't, she would have done the political thing and set up an investigation to review the data at a later date. But now, here, it was displayed in front of the entire mission control team. She'd probably doubted Sponder all along but had no proof that would enable her to do anything about it.

Sponder wasn't arrested yet, but I was exhilarated. This wasn't like flying in the *Phantom* with Kass. This was like my work on Earth. I dug up the data. Processed it. Analyzed it. Found the bad guys. Took them down.

Facts were facts. It was finding those facts that made catching the bad guys hard. I brought the truth to light, and I was damn good at it.

I would now, for the first time, expose the dark truth about someone I knew. Someone I could look in the eyes and enjoy watching them realize they'd been caught. It was also the first time someone's evil had affected me and someone I loved.

On Earth, my job had been real but not personal.

Now, this? Sponder? It was more than personal.

I started with the information I'd retrieved on the *Phantom*.

"I believe you've heard of Delegate Rainhart? The traitor to all of Velerion? The person responsible for the decimation of the Starfighter fleet?"

I thought a hush fell over the room for a moment.

"Yes," Jennix said. The one word was taut with tension.

Everyone knew what Rainhart had done. I didn't know how widespread that knowledge might be because I was new to the planet, but apparently he was infamous.

"Captain Sponder is in league with Rainhart?"

"That's outrageous!" Sponder shouted. "I'm here leading Group Two shuttle teams, offering valuable resources to Xenon. How can you not question her data? Her pair bond is a cheat and a liar. Guards, arrest him. Again. Arrest them both."

Guards appeared behind Kass. I felt movement behind me and turned to see two less than enthusiastic members of the control room's security detail. They hadn't touched me, yet. Sponder opened his mouth to shout more orders, but Jennix held up a hand.

"Wait," she called. The guards stilled, holding off for additional orders from Jennix, who outranked Sponder. "Continue, MCS Becker."

I nodded. "On the screen, you can clearly see the trail of data that proves they've been working on multiple projects together for well over a year. I found encrypted files with structural drawings and maps of a massive base of some kind as well as a large building on the surface of Velerion. It looks like a giant meeting place of some kind. The Hall of Records?"

"Oh shit," the other general said. "Queen Raya is going to take out the Hall of Records?"

"What is that?" I asked.

Kass blinked hard, and I saw him brighten as he

thought of a way to explain it to me. "It's like a country's capitol building on Earth. All the lawmakers are there, like a Velerion senate."

Jennix began to rub her forehead in a subtle sign of distress. "There are many secret passageways, underground tunnels, and decentralized power stations to protect it from a direct assault. We knew she'd received her information about the Starfighter base from Delegate Rainhart. But if Queen Raya has the structural details for the Hall of Records as well?"

"General, this is—"

Jennix looked to Sponder. "Silence."

Sponder was fighting for his life now and forged ahead despite the general's warning. "If he falsified his records for the training program, what makes you think his pair bond isn't doing the same now? To protect him?"

"Because MCS Becker didn't know Velerion was real until two days ago. The time stamp on the data collection indicates the time when MCS Remeas was in the brig."

"And in the *Phantom,* General," I added. "I discovered the link to Rainhart on the way to the moon base."

She glanced at the second time stamp and

nodded. Then continued with Sponder. "You put Remeas in the brig yourself. Becker wouldn't have had time to learn the history of Delegate Rainhart and fake reports. And since she was expecting Lieutenant Markus to be her mission partner, they certainly couldn't plan this en route."

Sponder's face was turning a dark shade of red.

"I have sorted multiple threads of conversations between Rainhart and Sponder as well as detailed instances of report tampering. The ghost trail Sponder left behind while inserting *Starfighter Training Academy* mission modifications is included as well. As for today's mission, my mech team and I both saw Captain Sponder exiting the *Phantom* a few minutes before takeoff. And our ship wasn't hit by the enemy; it was blown up from within."

Jennix clenched her jaw. "Comms," she called again. "Analyze data in the *Phantom's* docking bay, previous three hours. Can you confirm reports of Captain Sponder's presence near the *Phantom*."

"No data found," the AI voice responded.

The corner of Sponder's mouth tipped up.

"May I, General?" Kass asked.

Jennix nodded.

"Comms," Kass called. "Analyze data in docking bay, previous three hours. Report and display the last person to approach the *Phantom* prior to Starfighter MCS Becker's arrival."

"Processing. Data visible on screen six."

The image showed Mech Vintis, one of the mechanics, placing something beneath the weapons panel. But his uniform looked odd and the image was a bit blurry.

"Comms, locate Mech Vintis at the time this recording was taken."

"Processing. Data visible on screen six."

A view of the docking bay popped up on the screen. Mech Vintis and Mech Arria were sitting at a small work station, laughing and enjoying a meal together while taking a break from their duties.

"Vintis could not be in two places at once," Kass said.

"And I personally saw Captain Sponder walk off my ship." I couldn't help myself; I wanted to jump on Sponder's back and strangle him. "You bastard."

Kass interrupted before I could say more, which was probably a good thing as I was really close to acting on my instincts.

"Comms, track Captain's Sponder's location five minutes prior to that time."

"Processing. Data visible on screen six."

I held my breath until I saw Captain Sponder

with Commissioner Gaius enter the Starfighter docking bay. Sponder carried something small. He walked across the docking bay toward the *Phantom* as Gaius spoke to the Mechs. Vintis asked Sponder if he required assistance. Sponder declined.

We all watched Sponder cover the distance to our ship. A few paces away, he looked up into the camera and the screen blurred, his clothing changed to that of Mech Vintis.

The new, blurry version of Vintis/Sponder walked straight up to the *Phantom* and disappeared inside.

Several minutes later he reappeared on the ramp, still a confusing, blurred image of Vintis/Sponder, when I appeared on the screen.

I remembered it perfectly. I looked at him, glared, and asked what the hell he was doing on my ship. He'd said he was there to apologize about Kass, let me know he was saving me from a cheat and a liar, and to have a good mission.

But on the screen Vintis and I had that conversation instead.

Sponder might be an ass, but he was more than adequate at covering his tracks in the digital world.

Until me.

"I remember that conversation, General Jennix.

And it was not Mech Vintis I spoke to, but Captain Sponder. I give you my word."

There it was. Proof that Sponder had placed the bomb on the *Phantom*. The time stamp was when Kass had been in the brig and I was clearly on-screen, having a little chat about my pair bond.

"Sponder had no way of knowing I would escape the brig and go on the mission with Mia. He intended to kill my pair bond, General," Kass growled. He was coiled and ready to strike more than just Sponder's nose.

"I wanted to see your face when you found out she was dead," Sponder snapped, spittle flying.

Kass attacked then, punching Sponder so hard he fell to the ground. Kass jumped on him, pummeled him. "You don't fuck with my Mia," he said, each word followed by a brutal punch.

Jennix didn't say anything for a few seconds, but then waved her hand to have the guards pull Kass off. Sponder was conscious but bloody and in bad shape. The guards hoisted Sponder to his feet and had to hold him up.

"You'd have gotten away with everything," I told Sponder. "No one would have suspected you of being in allegiance with Rainhart. It was your hatred for Kass that gave you away. You should have let him join the MCS without complaint. He was your downfall."

"Take Sponder away," Jennix ordered. "Transport him immediately to the lockdown station on Velerion. Maximum security." She frowned. "I'll deal with Commissioner Gaius later." She turned to look at me. "What about the commissioner? You find anything on him? Is he a traitor as well?"

I shook my head. "Not that I can tell. Just a man with an asshole for a nephew."

"Well, at least that's something," she muttered. "General Aryk?"

"Yes, General."

She looked to the other leader, who blinked, stunned at what had just happened. "Aryk, we need to finish the mission."

General Aryk nodded. "I will take control of Group Two. We will see the liberation of Xenon a success." He looked to us. "Good work, MCS pair."

"Yes, good work," Jennix added, then frowned. "I'm going to assume the records showing you cheated in the training program are false, as Starfighter MCS Becker has attested. However, I have a mission to run. You are ordered to remain in your quarters until a full review can be completed."

Kass grinned. It was the first time he'd done so

since he'd kicked the replacement pilot, Markus or something, out of the *Phantom* and hopped in with me.

"Affirmative, General. We will obey your command." Kass looked to me. Winked. "With pleasure."

13

A GUARD ESCORTED us to our quarters, but unlike the last time, when I was taken away by one, I wasn't in restraints. No weapons were out and ready to stun me. No smart remarks or shoving occurred. And— very different—this time I held Mia's hand, even raised it to my lips and kissed her knuckles a time or two.

She'd saved my ass. If not for her, no one would have caught Sponder's lies and exposed him as a traitor. My mind reeled with the information that he'd been working with Delegate Rainhart this

entire time, that he'd also been responsible for the
attack on the Starfighter base. That he'd helped
Queen Raya take Xenon prisoner, helped the Dark
Fleet target Velerion with the IPBMs. Why would he
do such a thing? He was Velerion himself. His family
was wealthy. His uncle was a commissioner in the
Hall of Records.

I squeezed Mia's hand. "I can't believe Sponder is
a traitor. I knew he was an ass, but—I don't understand what drove him to betray his own people."

Mia's turn. She lifted my hand to her lips and
kissed me. "Sometimes people don't make sense."

Well, that was the truth. "They'll execute him, if
what you found was true."

"It's true." She sounded completely confident,
sure of herself, and very, very sexy.

Mia had given General Jennix and General Aryk
more than enough proof to convict Sponder of
everything we'd claimed and then some. It was over.
Not the mission to save Xenon and to rid the
universe of IPBMs, but our fight to be together, to
prove ourselves worthy of our uniforms. We would
not be torn apart. I'd told Mia that from the first time
we met in her place of employment on Earth. She
was mine.

Forever.

I never expected Sponder to be more than just a nuisance to me. And a horrible leader. But Mia had found not only the truth about me, but the depth of his evil. Of course Mia had found it. No one else had and that was why Sponder had gone unnoticed, free to work with Delegate Rainhart in an unlimited capacity. Time would reveal the extent of his traitorous actions, but someone else would dig for those details. Mia had given them the trail to follow. That was all they were going to get, because Mia would be busy with me. In the short term, she would be busy being pleasured. I would see her rewarded for her actions. I would also ensure she was whole. Alive. Safe.

My heart seized at the idea of her dying in a fiery explosion of Sponder's making. It would have been as he'd said. Horrible. I would not have survived if she'd been killed. And with the other pilot trying to control the *Phantom* during the crash? I'd barely managed to save us, and I had more training in that ship than anyone on Velerion. I was a Starfighter for a reason. With Lieutenant Markus flying when that bomb went off, I would have lost her.

Being alive and in the brig would have been a

fate worse than death. Even if the charges against me for cheating had been proven false, I would not have been whole. I never would have forgiven myself for not being on that ship next to her. For not being there when she needed me.

For allowing her to die alone.

When the door to our quarters slid closed behind us, I locked the door, closing us away from all interruptions, and pulled her into my arms. Held her in a fierce hug.

Felt her heartbeat. Her breath.

"Kass," she whispered.

"I know," I replied, kissing the top of her head.

"Now. It has to be now," she murmured.

I couldn't agree with her more, but we were still wearing our flight suits, dust and debris from the crash, the smell of burning metal and rock draping over us both like a cloud. Dropping to my knees, I yanked and pulled to remove her flight suit and boots. When she stood naked before me, I placed a kiss in the center of her abdomen and leaned my forehead into her body. I inhaled the scent of her feminine heat and reveled in the feeling of her fingers stroking my scalp, combing my hair. Holding me to her.

"I almost lost you."

"We almost lost each other."

I wrapped my arms around her waist and held on tightly, sinking into her, memorizing everything about her. Scent. Touch. Softness of her skin. Gentleness of her hands. She sighed. "It won't be the last time, Kass. We are Starfighters. We aren't going to be sitting behind a desk." She grabbed a fistful of my hair and tilted my head up to meet her gaze. "And I don't want to be. I want to be out there, making a difference. With you. And if we die, we die together."

This woman was going to be the death of me one way or the other. At the moment I feared my heart was going to burst inside my chest, the explosion of emotion inside me crippling and painful. "I love you."

"I love you, too."

"Live together. Fight together. Die together."

"Exactly." She grinned. "Are you in or are you out?"

"Oh, I'm in. And so are you." I stood in a flash and lifted her off her feet, throwing her over my shoulder as I marched us both to the bathing room. I set her on her feet in the stall, and she started the water as I stepped out of my flight suit and boots.

Hot water streaming, we washed one another in

record time. The second I had her soft and wet and clean, had inspected every inch of her for injuries and found nothing but a few bruises, I dropped to my knees and used my hand on her stomach to hold her back pressed to the shower wall. She fought for balance, but I had no more self-control. I needed her. "Now. I need you now."

"Kass," she said again, this time on a moan. My intention was clear. Her fingers tangled in my hair, and I looked up at her.

"Now," I repeated, then licked into her. It was hard to do with her legs so close together, but her clit was hard and poking from its hood as if eager for me. With my other hand, I cupped her bare pussy in my palm, slipped two fingers deep inside her body, and made it my mission to get her off. With fingers and tongue, I pushed her toward orgasm without mercy. There was no teasing. I was focused, quick, and precise. I knew what she liked. Knew where to touch and stroke and lick.

She didn't fight me, gasping and crying out as I made her come.

My cock was hard. Aching to fill her. I denied myself any satisfaction. Yet.

She screamed her second release, her knees buckling. Her pussy gushing with her essence. I drank it down, savored the way her inner walls rippled around my fingers, the way her entire body shook, knees weak, gasping for air. Mia was out of control. Mine.

Yes.

Fuck, yes. She held nothing back, gave me everything. Trust. Love. Surrender. She. Was. Mine.

Completely.

———

Mia

KASS STOOD with a smug grin on his face.

Yeah, he was pleased with himself.

He should be.

That had been epic. And I knew we were far from done.

Kass dunked his head under the water as I recovered enough to reach for him. I pulled him to me for a kiss that went on and on. I wanted to merge our bodies into one being. Hold him this close forever. He was mine. I would fight to protect him until my dying breath, and I knew he'd do the same for me.

Bonded pair. I understood what that really meant now. Bonded. One.

I was thankful to Jennix and her order to remain in our quarters. Based on what Kass had just done to me, he had big plans to take advantage of our alone time.

Turning off the water, I tugged him out of the shower and toward the towels. I took my time drying him off because... yeah, I had plans, too.

"I can't decide what turns me on more, you in uniform in the cockpit flying the *Phantom,* or you naked," I said, taking a bit of extra time to gently rub the towel along his hard cock.

"I prefer both in the cockpit and naked. That was epic," he replied.

Our pace was slow for once. We weren't frantic for each other. Okay, we were, but after everything we'd been through, savoring this alone time was nice, too. Maybe I wasn't in a hurry because he'd taken the edge off my need with his mouth. But the bulge was a sign that he had yet to ease his battle desire. Almost dying—twice—was one thing. But we'd also had to fight Sponder. Fight to be together. And we'd won.

We were together. Nothing could keep us apart now. And if anyone interrupted us... they'd have to deal with me. Because house arrest meant lots of sexy times.

"Only if you don't set me down on top of the comms controls next time," I muttered, then giggled when he tickled me.

He took his time, dried me off at a leisurely pace, but as he touched and rubbed and explored more and more of my bare skin, I became more eager.

"I need you," I admitted.

His gaze met mine. I saw the heat there. The need.

"Again?"

I nodded. "I can't get enough of you. I'll never get enough."

His face softened at that, if just for a moment.

"I need you, too," he replied. "In bed. With your legs parted so I can see every gorgeous part of you."

My inner walls clenched at his words, and I didn't wait but turned and headed toward the bed.

A hand came down on my ass. I spun about as the sting bloomed and turned into heat. Kass stood there, naked, arms crossed over his chest, cock thrust toward me like a soldier standing at attention. He was grinning, definitely pleased with himself.

"What was that for?" I asked.

He looked at my butt, tilted his head. "I like seeing my mark on you."

I huffed in fake indignation when the truth was, that sting had traveled straight to my core, tightened my nipples, made my body wake up in a way I'd never felt before. I wanted more.

He stepped close, reached down, and cupped my pussy. "You're drenched. You loved it."

I tipped my chin up, ready to deny it. But this was Kass. He would give me anything I wanted. Anything I needed. Anything at all without judgment or hesitation. He was mine.

"I did. And your mouth on me, too."

His eyes flared. "Noted."

He licked his fingers of my essence, then growled.

"Change of plans. On the bed. All fours. Ass up."

This time, I turned a little slower.

"Gorgeous, you're getting your ass spanked no matter what. Don't be shy now."

I set a knee on the bed, then crawled up into the center, positioned myself as he wanted. Arched my back. This stuck my butt out, and he could see everything. I'd never been a prude, but I was *very* exposed. He could see all of me. When I looked over my shoulder, saw the way his jaw was clenched, the way he looked on the edge of losing control, almost feral, I basked in my power over him.

I wiggled my butt, and he broke his stare. He moved quicker now, settling onto the bed in a way that confused me. A few seconds later I nearly moaned in anticipation because he'd flipped onto his back, his head between my thighs so I straddled his face.

"*Scheisse,*" I breathed.

When his hands cupped my ass to pull me down so he could lock his lips around my clit and suck my flesh, I moaned. Writhed. Rode his face. It didn't take long to come. There had been so much buildup. So much need.

I was wild and rocking on him as he used his mouth and tongue to get me off. My clit had never been so happy to see someone.

After I screamed his name, lost in the pleasure only Kass could wring from me, he moved again. Kneeling behind me, he spanked me.

"I should punish you for being too gorgeous. Too smart." His palm struck my ass with a sharp sting that made me wiggle. Again. And again. "Too brave."

My ass heated up. One side, then the other. My body rocked forward with each heated smack on my ass, my breasts swinging below me, nipples so hard they ached.

More. I wanted more.

"You are mine, Mia. *Mine.*"

One more smack and then he was at my entrance, the broad crown nudging, parting, then thrusting deep.

"Yes!" I cried as my walls rippled to accommodate him.

"Gods," he gritted out. "Fuck, you're perfect."

He pounded into me. Hard. Deep. As if chasing something.

My breasts swayed, and I rubbed the sensitive nipples along the bedding as I pushed back into his thrusts, met him. Took him deep. Demanded more.

I gripped the bedding. Held on. I was close to coming. So close. I reached beneath me for my clit. If I just rubbed it once or twice, I would come again.

Kass brushed my hand away, then pulled out.

"Wha—" The word was caught in my throat as I was flipped onto my back. Kass pushed my legs wide, looked his fill, then settled between them and thrust deep, took me again.

I looked up into his dark eyes. He was watching me as he filled me. His pelvis rubbed against my clit, and I knew what he was doing now. He wanted to watch me come. Wanted to witness the moment I surrendered, lost myself to the pleasure he gave me.

He didn't have to wait long. With my hands digging into his ass, I came again. It was a rolling, searing release, prolonged by the way his cock rubbed and stroked secret places inside me.

Sweat glistened on my skin as I bucked and arched beneath him. Pleasure burst from me, but I kept looking at Kass. Held his gaze. Let him see exactly what he did to me, what he meant to me. I didn't want to break the connection because we were together in this. In all things. Forever.

"Your turn," I whispered.

Kass didn't slow his hips, only lost his rhythm, giving over to his basest needs. "Your pleasure is my pleasure, Mia. You are my life. My heart. You saved me," he said.

"And you saved me right back," I added on a moan.

He roared then, holding himself deep, filling me with his seed.

I came again, softly, a gentle little ripple of heat that made my body milk him dry.

We'd given everything to be together. We burned hot. We fought dirty. We claimed wild. We would never be tamed. Never be alone. Never walk away or betray one another. We were a pair bond. We were one.

Our rebel natures might get us in trouble here and there, but I wouldn't have it any other way.

Kass was mine. If the Velerions didn't like that? Well, too damn bad.

I was keeping him.

e were under house arrest for three days. I'd never been in jail before, nor did I want to be, but being stuck with Kass with nothing to do but be naked and get to know each other—*really* well—wasn't all that bad.

It had been incredible. Besides the number of orgasms we'd had—I'd lost count after a while—we'd talked. Discovered we were more compatible than we'd ever imagined.

The one thing we hadn't been able to do was for me to learn about my new home world. Velerion was where I lived now, and all I'd seen was the inside of the *Resolution* and on missions. So when General Jennix cleared Kass of the accusations against him—

except for the hacking into the *Starfighter Training Academy* candidate program—we were free to go.

To Velerion.

Xenon had been successfully liberated from the Dark Fleet. The IPBMs that remained had been destroyed. The factory would revert back to ore production. Xenon as a planet would return to normal. To peace. Without a moon base, which had been completely destroyed. It was undecided yet if it would be rebuilt.

But that wasn't for me or Kass to analyze. We were given leave along with Jamie and Alex, and we met them on Velerion.

So here we were, just outside of Eos Station where Kass used to be based, walking in a park. With people. And babies. And pets that looked like small polar bears complete with long claws, fuzzy white fur, and saddles for the children to ride.

Saddles. On bears.

The ambling creatures had bright blue eyes, not Earth bear brown, and they were about the size of a large dog, but still. Bears.

"They are very protective of their families and are considered wonderful pets." Kass's hand was at the small of my back, and I reveled in the momentary normal feeling of walking with him, in a park, with children playing and bears rolling in the grass with one another as wistful, smiling parents watched with the same besotted look I'd seen thousands of times on Earth.

Almost made me want children. Almost.

Kass kissed my temple. "I enjoy watching the little ones the most."

Scheisse. "I don't want to be a mother." I had things to do, and being a mother was not one of them. "I was never one of those little girls that played with baby dolls and pretended to be a mother. It's not for me, Kass."

He froze. "I want you. I want to fight to protect my people. I have no need to be a father." He kissed me again. "We're warriors, my Mia. A battleship is no place for children. We fight. We protect. We die." He nodded to a very small girl, perhaps two years old, who had tackled her bear pet. The adorable duo was rolling around and growling, the little girl treating her bear like she would a puppy. "They play."

Thank God. I hadn't even thought about Kass wanting children before now, but the relief I felt was like bubbles in my blood and the blue and green sky looked brighter, the flowers more beautiful, the heat of Kassius at my back like home. I'd never been this content on Earth. Here we were, stealing maybe an hour after facing down an interplanetary traitor and two war generals, and I was giddy.

I was never giddy.

Then again, I had never walked on an alien planet before. The moon base was one thing, but it had been barren and uninhabited and scary as hell. This was peaceful. Safe. And beautiful. Flowers of every color I'd ever seen, and some I hadn't, blossomed from well-groomed beds. The grass was soft and sank under our combat boots to spring up again like a sponge once we'd passed. Small insects similar to bees buzzed from flower to flower, their pearlescent green and blue bodies like floating gemstones sparkling in Vega's warm light. Jamie noticed the new colors as well and pointed to one of the more radiant, oddly colored blooms. "What is that?"

"A flower?" Alex answered.

"No. What color is that?"

Kass wrapped his arms around me from behind, and I leaned into him. "That is a Vega Star Blossom." He squeezed me. "Have you never seen that color before?"

"No." I hadn't. I couldn't even begin to describe it.

"Must be your cipher implants. When fully integrated, they enhance all your senses, not just your hearing and language abilities. They also increase reaction time, which is very helpful in battle."

I didn't want to think about the weird nanotech crawling around inside my brain. Yes, understanding and speaking the language was helpful, but I did not like the idea of the implants. Maybe, one day, I'd grow accustomed. For now I ignored it and focused on the little girl and her gentle bear who were lying on the ground facing one another, nose to nose, as she patted the bear's face.

That was one patient animal.

Jamie and Alex had wandered to look at another section of blooms while I was content to stand and sway in Kass's arms.

The little girl glanced up and giggled as her older sister came flying through the park to join them, her much longer legs pumping at full speed until she reached them. "Mother says it's time to eat." She was probably eight or nine and very sure of herself.

"Not hungry, are we?" The little one kissed her bear.

The older sister put her hands on her hips and tilted her head in a bossy stance I recognized all too easily. "Mother says—" The elder sister looked up, and her gaze landed on us. She froze. "Starfighters."

"Where?" The baby scrambled to her feet, and the lumbering bear rolled onto its side before managing to place itself between the two girls and stare at us.

"Right there!" The older girl pointed, and her baby sister finally looked up and registered our presence.

"Do you want to run?" Kass whispered. "Now's your only chance."

Run? From children? "Don't be ridiculous." I pulled free from Kass's arms and walked slowly toward the girls so as not to scare them. "Hello. I'm Mia. What's your name?"

"Starfighter MCS Mia?" the older girl shouted with excitement and glanced behind me to Kass. "Are you Kassius Remeas, the rebel hacker?"

I glanced over my shoulder to find Kass now ambling toward us with a grin on his face. "Am I famous, then?"

"Yes! My mother said you broke the rules, but Father said we needed you, so it's allowed." She scrunched her nose up at him, and I honestly could not tell the difference between these people and humans. "But only for Starfighters. We can't break rules like you, or we'll be in trouble."

"Big trouble," the little one confirmed.

"Can I touch it?" The older girl pointed at the silver swirl on my Starfighter uniform, so I knelt in front of them, careful of the bear creature, and both girls walked forward without a hint a fear and reached for me.

"I love this," the little one said.

"Thank you."

The older girl ran her fingers along the emblem, then reached up to my neck. When she couldn't see the mark there, she walked around behind me, lifting my hair from my neck until she found it. Small, sticky fingers followed as the two ran their hands over my skin.

"Someday I want to be a Starfighter."

"Me, too."

The older girl looked at her baby sister. "Mother says you are going to work with animals because you can talk to them."

"Yeah."

"I can't."

The tiny girl giggled like she had a secret as she stepped back and placed her arm over the bear's neck. "Orion likes you."

"Is Orion your bear?"

"He's not a bear. He's Orion."

Right. Toddler logic. "I like him, too."

The older girl remained at my shoulder, transfixed by the marking there.

"Leave the Starfighters alone, ladies," a man's voice called out, and I looked away from the gentle eyes of the mini polar bear to find a man and woman —I assumed to be the girls' parents—nearly upon us.

"They're all right."

"Orion likes Mia."

"I'm sure he does," their mother confirmed.

I stood slowly and turned to find not just the girls' parents, but a gathering of at least fifty adults and children closing in on our location. I looked over to Kass, who had his arms crossed and was grinning at me.

"Tried to warn you."

"What are they doing?" I asked.

"You are famous, Mia."

"Famous?" What the hell was he talking about?

"Look." He pointed to the opposite side of the grassy area where Alex and Jamie were surrounded by people as well.

"Why?"

"You're a Starfighter, my Mia. Hero of the planet. Last hope of winning the war. Every person here is counting on us to save them."

Scheisse. Fighting? Fine. Hacking into Dark Fleet systems? No problem. Staring into the eyes of hundreds of people who thought I was a savior of some kind? No. I was no one special. I said as much.

Kass wrapped his arm around my waist as we were surrounded by well-wishers, fans, and curious children. Seemed most of them worked at Eos Station and kept up-to-date on the war effort. Queen Raya had been gaining ground for months, until Jamie's arrival. And now mine.

"We got the Xenon back because of them!" one of the men shouted. The crowd took up his chant. "Xenon! Xenon!"

The older girl still stood close, and she threw her arms around my waist. Squeezed. Hard. "Thank you. Velia and Camillia live there!"

"Who?" I asked.

"Their cousins. We have not been able to find out —" The girls' mother cleared her throat. "My sister and her family work on Xenon. We have not been able to communicate with them since the Dark Fleet took over."

"I'm sorry." I had no idea what to say.

Kass's soothing voice calmed the entire crowd. "I'm sure they are all right. We will know within a few hours. They needed workers who knew how to operate the systems there. And they are free now."

The girl squeezed me tighter as Kass and I spent the next half hour smiling and greeting strangers who seemed to know everything about us. One man even mentioned the fact that I was from Earth.

"Do you know where Earth is?" I asked.

"Never heard of it before, but I hope there are a lot more of you coming."

Lily would be next. I had no doubt. After that? Based on the millions of people playing the game? I answered him with confidence. "There will be. I promise."

A SPECIAL THANK YOU TO MY READERS...

Want more? I've got *hidden* bonus content on my web site *exclusively* for those on my <u>mailing list.</u>

If you are already on my email list, you don't need to do a thing! Simply scroll to the bottom of my newsletter emails and click on the *super-secret* link.

Not a member? What are you waiting for? In addition to ALL of my bonus content (great new stuff will be added regularly) you will be the first to hear about my newest release the second it hits the stores—AND you will get a free book as a special welcome gift.

Sign up now! http://freescifiromance.com

FIND YOUR INTERSTELLAR MATCH!

YOUR mate is out there. Take the test today and discover your perfect match. Are you ready for a sexy alien mate (or two)?

VOLUNTEER NOW!

interstellarbridesprogram.com

DO YOU LOVE AUDIOBOOKS?

Grace Goodwin's books are now available as
audiobooks...everywhere.

LET'S TALK!

Interested in joining my **Sci-Fi Squad**? Meet new like-minded sci-fi romance fanatics and chat with Grace! Get excerpts, cover reveals and sneak peeks before anyone else. Be part of a private Facebook group that shares pictures and fun news! Join here:

https://www.facebook.com/groups/scifisquad/

Want to talk about Grace Goodwin books with others? Join the **SPOILER ROOM** and spoil away! Your GG BFFs are waiting! (And so is Grace) Join here:

https://www.facebook.com/groups/ggspoilerroom/

GET A FREE BOOK!

JOIN MY MAILING LIST TO BE THE FIRST TO KNOW OF NEW RELEASES, FREE BOOKS, SPECIAL PRICES AND OTHER AUTHOR GIVEAWAYS.

http://freescifiromance.com

ALSO BY GRACE GOODWIN

Starfighter Training Academy

The First Starfighter

Starfighter Command

Elite Starfighter

Interstellar Brides® Program: The Beasts

Bachelor Beast

Maid for the Beast

Beauty and the Beast

The Beasts Boxed Set

Interstellar Brides® Program

Assigned a Mate

Mated to the Warriors

Claimed by Her Mates

Taken by Her Mates

Mated to the Beast

Mastered by Her Mates

Tamed by the Beast

Mated to the Vikens

Her Mate's Secret Baby

Mating Fever

Her Viken Mates

Fighting For Their Mate

Her Rogue Mates

Claimed By The Vikens

The Commanders' Mate

Matched and Mated

Hunted

Viken Command

The Rebel and the Rogue

Rebel Mate

Surprise Mates

Interstellar Brides® Program Boxed Set - Books 6-8

Interstellar Brides® Program Boxed Set - Books 9-12

Interstellar Brides® Program Boxed Set - Books 13-16

Interstellar Brides® Program: The Colony

Surrender to the Cyborgs

Mated to the Cyborgs

Cyborg Seduction

Her Cyborg Beast

Cyborg Fever

Rogue Cyborg

Cyborg's Secret Baby

Her Cyborg Warriors

The Colony Boxed Set 1

The Colony Boxed Set 2

Interstellar Brides® Program: The Virgins

The Alien's Mate

His Virgin Mate

Claiming His Virgin

His Virgin Bride

His Virgin Princess

The Virgins - Complete Boxed Set

Interstellar Brides® Program: Ascension Saga

Ascension Saga, book 1

Ascension Saga, book 2

Ascension Saga, book 3

Trinity: Ascension Saga - Volume 1

Ascension Saga, book 4

Ascension Saga, book 5

Ascension Saga, book 6

Faith: Ascension Saga - Volume 2

Ascension Saga, book 7

Ascension Saga, book 8

Ascension Saga, book 9

Destiny: Ascension Saga - Volume 3

Other Books

Their Conquered Bride

Wild Wolf Claiming: A Howl's Romance

ABOUT GRACE

Grace Goodwin is a USA Today and international bestselling author of Sci-Fi and Paranormal romance with more than one million books sold. Grace's titles are available worldwide in multiple languages in ebook, print and audio formats. Two best friends, one left-brained, the other right-brained, make up the award winning writing duo that is Grace Goodwin. They are both mothers, escape room enthusiasts, avid readers and intrepid defenders of their preferred beverages. (There may or may not be an ongoing tea vs. coffee war occurring during their daily communications.) Grace loves to hear from readers! All of Grace's books can be read as sexy, stand-alone adventures. But be careful, she likes her heroes hot and her love scenes hotter. You have been warned...

www.gracegoodwin.com
gracegoodwinauthor@gmail.com

Printed in Great Britain
by Amazon